John Stuart

Memoir of the Late Alexander Henry Rhind of Sibster

John Stuart

Memoir of the Late Alexander Henry Rhind of Sibster

ISBN/EAN: 9783337372118

Printed in Europe, USA, Canada, Australia, Japan

Cover: Foto ©Raphael Reischuk / pixelio.de

More available books at **www.hansebooks.com**

MEMOIR

OF THE LATE

ALEXANDER HENRY RHIND,

OF SIBSTER.

BY

JOHN STUART,

SECRETARY OF THE SOCIETY OF ANTIQUARIES OF SCOTLAND.

EDINBURGH:
PRINTED BY NEILL AND COMPANY.

MDCCCLXIV.

THE substance of the following Memoir was read at the Anniversary Meeting of the Society of Antiquaries in November last. At the request of the Council, the paper has been considerably enlarged by the introduction of farther selections from Mr Rhind's correspondence, principally from a series of letters addressed by him to two of his friends, the Rev. John Earle, Rector of Swanswick near Bath, and Dr J. Barnard Davis, one of the editors of "Crania Britannica," which these gentlemen readily placed at my disposal.

Mr Bremner, the literary executor of Mr Rhind, having put into my possession the manuscripts left by his relative, I have made various selections from them, which are now printed in the Memoir.

The portrait of Mr Rhind has been successfully engraved by Mr Robert C. Bell, from a photograph taken in 1860, belonging to Mr Alexander Kincaid Mackenzie, the brother-in-law of Mr Rhind, which seems to me to preserve a faithful and pleasing likeness of the original, as he appeared in his later years.

J. S.

MARCH, 1864.

MEMOIR

OF

ALEXANDER HENRY RHIND.

THE late Alexander Henry Rhind was the only surviving son of Josiah Rhind of Sibster, banker in Wick. He was born on the 26th July 1833, and during his earlier years pursued his studies at the Pulteneytown Academy, under the tuition of Mr Andrew Scott, now Professor of Oriental Languages in the University of Aberdeen. He then proceeded to the University of Edinburgh, where he became a student in the class of Natural History in the session of 1848-49, and in the class of Natural Philosophy in the session of 1849-50 ; but even when at College, his early taste for historical pursuits displayed itself, and, as he wrote to me many years afterwards, he then attended the lectures of Professor Cosmo Innes on Scottish history and antiquities, delivered in the University in the winter of 1849-50 ; "and they appealed" (he writes) " so naturally to my then growing old-world tastes, that I was an unfailingly regular attendant."

Some of his common-place books of this period are preserved, which begin with notes of College lectures, but soon merge into extracts from works on the early history and topography of Scotland, especially of the shire of Caithness, with details of Picts' Houses and cairns in his own district.

In March 1851 he was occupied in opening a set of remarkable cairns at Yarrows, and other localities, in the southern corner of the parish of Wick ; and about the same time he translated from the German a work on "The National Knowledge of Antiquities in Germany, and Notes of a Tour," by J. T. A. Worsaae.

In the summer of this year he visited the Great Exhibition in London, and thereafter proceeded to a tour on the Continent, which occupied him for several months. In the course of it he passed through the Low Countries, Switzerland, Italy, Austria, Saxony, Prussia, and Denmark, and visited all the remarkable museums of antiquities in these countries.

My first intercourse with Mr Rhind occurred in the early part of 1852. He had been made aware of my inquiries for examples of sculptured pillar-stones and crosses, and accordingly sent me rubbings of the curious slab at Ulbster, of which a drawing will be found in my volume "The Sculptured Stones of Scotland," printed for the Spalding Club. The patience and care of Mr Rhind in removing the coating of hard impacted vegetable growth which covered and obscured the figures on this monument, involving the work of several days, were singularly in harmony with the accurate habits of research which his maturer years developed, and which he carried into all his pursuits.

In December of this year, he was elected a Fellow of the Society of Antiquaries of Scotland, and in the course of the session he presented to the Museum two remarkable stone vessels found near Wick. In May 1853, he prepared a paper, of which an abstract is printed in the Proceedings (vol. i. p. 182), as " an attempt to define how far the Cymric encroached upon the Gaelic branch of the early Celtic population of North Britain." This paper furnishes abundant evidence of wide reading and careful independent thought.

About this time Mr Rhind devoted much attention to the systematic examination of a Pict's house at Kettleburn in his native county, carried out by workmen under his own eye and directions. A paper appears in the "Archæological Journal" for 1853, in which Mr Rhind gave an account of this examination, and in 1854, the whole collection of archæological relics and osteological remains found in the Pict's house were presented to our Society with a descriptive memoir, which is printed in the "Proceedings," vol. i. p. 264.

In August 1854, Mr Rhind addressed the following characteristic letter to the Crystal Palace Company, suggesting to them the propriety of erecting models of certain early British remains in their grounds at Sydenham :—

J. GROVE, Esq.,
Secretary to the Crystal Palace Co.

SIBSTER, near WICK, *August* 16, 1854.

" SIR,—I am not aware whether it has occurred to the Directors of the Crystal Palace, that it might be very desirable to include among the contemplated additions to its attractions, restorations, or, I should rather say, copies of certain primeval British remains, which could not fail to be universally instructing, and at the same time highly promotive of the advancement of archæological science. If this suggestion has not already presented itself to those officially connected with the undertaking in question, I would venture to urge, that it is worthy of consideration ; and perhaps you will permit me to state my reasons for believing it to be so.

" It is true that we may search in vain among the rude antiquities of our own land for structures which have any artistic beauty to recommend them, or which could produce the dazzling effect of the restored antiquities of the East ; but then the gentlemen interested in the Sydenham Palace have wisely shown, as indeed they originally professed, that it is their design, not merely to gratify or educate the eye, but also to supply suggestive materials for intellectual information. It will not, therefore, I imagine, be an objection to British aboriginal remains, that in an ornamental point of view they would be deficient, since, as practical and really attractive instructors, their value would be undoubted. Nor does it seem altogether free from anomaly, that the visitors to the " great popular educator," as it has justly been termed, should have every facility for ascertaining how an Assyrian monarch was housed three thousand years ago, or for studying the sepulchral customs which prevailed on the banks of the Nile more than a millennium before our era, while no means whatever are afforded to enable them to form any idea of the manners and state of civilisation at those periods of their predecessors on British soil—their ancestors it may be.   That such means, were they once in existence, would be eagerly and extensively taken advantage of, can scarcely be questioned ; for even among the most unthinking sightseers— much more among those of ordinary intelligence—when the curiosity is once excited with respect to past ages, it involuntarily and naturally directs itself with special reference to one's native land.   Thus many, had they only the opportunity, would doubtless acquire sensible and rational views on the subject of our national archæology, in place of pre- vious ignorance or erroneous prejudices ; and I feel persuaded, that another and very important result would be a more general diffusion of a knowledge of the scientific value of archæological relics, and of the con- sequent necessity that exists for their more careful preservation.   A more efficient vehicle for the promulgation of this truth can scarcely be con- ceived than the Crystal Palace, which cannot fail to be visited by people of all classes from all parts of the country ; and I do believe that the information on this matter which they might there receive, would do much to prevent the wanton destruction of aboriginal antiquities, which those who have practical opportunities for research are so incessantly called upon to deplore.

" I hesitate to offer any observations respecting the details of the pro- posal I have indicated ; but it will be seen that I have been alluding more particularly to the erection of *fac similes* of specimens of the more remark- able types of those primeval British remains which are of an architectural or structural character.   Some models of weapons, implements, utensils, and ornaments, might certainly be well introduced for illustrative purposes ; but as these smaller relics are already collected, and can be seen else- where, it would scarcely be an object to bring together very many copies of them at Sydenham.   *There*, as I conceive, attention should be directed to that which cannot be attempted in ordinary museums—to the repro- duction of those remains which are even more vivid exponents of pri- meval manners than weapons or tools, and which are more generally appreciable by unscientific beholders.   For how much more readily is the curiosity satisfied by a sight of the dwelling, than by the mere inspec- tion of the rude implements of its occupants ; how much more vague are the ideas called up by the arrow-head, the spear, and the sword, than by the actual presence of the stronghold which these were used to defend ; how much more meagre are the teachings of the urn and the favourite arms or decorations of the deceased, than of the sepulchre in which these were deposited.   And we have dwellings still in excellent preservation, the most curious of which are perhaps the ' Pict's Houses,' hill forts still nearly perfect in all their details, cromlechs and chambered cairns, which have well resisted the influence of ages, leaving nothing for the imagination to supply.   To reproduce examples of these and of such like (which, were it found necessary, could be effected without much detriment even in the open air) could not involve any extravagant expenditure, as the materials and workmanship would be of the coarsest kind; and I feel assured, even after making large deductions for my own antiquarian predilections, that the outlay would be fully justified by the interest taken in its results.   I am the more confirmed in this belief, from having had occasion to observe more particularly at Copenhagen, and at the Dublin Exhibition, the deep attention which casual visitors, with no strongly developed archæological tastes, are disposed to bestow on good collections even of the minor relics, which, as I have already implied, are not calculated to be so popularly significant or attractive as restorations of the character I have indicated.   Nor would it be the general public alone that would benefit by such reproductions, although this, of course, under the circumstances, would be the primary object, but scientific antiquaries, both native and foreign, and especially the latter, would find them of very considerable service ; as they would thus have an opportunity of examining in detail primeval structures which otherwise they would never see except on paper, since it might not be convenient for many of them to make pilgrimages to remote districts in Scotland or Ireland, where the finest examples of the remains in question are preserved.   This last consideration is, however, as I have said, of secondary importance, as the Directors, I doubt not, desire to make it their first care to provide that which shall be popularly available ; but even with this end only in view, and leaving out of sight the contingent advantages I have pointed out, still I would hope that it may be deemed advisable to reproduce at least some specimens of our national remains—of only a single dwelling and a single tomb—as a means of enabling every one to know something of primeval Britain.

" Conceiving that the Directors of the Crystal Palace Company will not regard as an intrusion any such suggestion as the above, when offered from proper motives and with becoming respect, I take the liberty to address them through you, and to request that you will be so obliging as to bring under their notice the subject of this letter.—I have the honour to be, Sir, yours faithfully."

Mr Rhind gave evidence of his diligent inquiries into the early History of Scotland in an article which appeared in the " Retrospective Review " for February 1853, under the title of " Early Scottish History and its Exponents." He chose as his text-book the well-known "Critical Essay" of Thomas Innes, and the following passage contains his opinion of that work :—

" It is not, of course, our intention to hold up the ' Critical Essay' as an unapproachable model of perfection, though candour must admit that few disquisitions of its kind can advantageously be compared with it. The section set apart for the elucidation of Scottish history, properly so called, is especially deserving of praise, from the comprehensiveness of its mode of treatment ; and the chapters allotted to the Picts are also valuable, though ethnologically we decline to recognise them as the standard of our faith. After making such an avowal, it may perhaps be expected by some that we should enter on the great battle-field of the Pictish controversy ; but on this occasion, having neither space nor inclination to do so, we have carefully and designedly eschewed this exciting subject, with the view of confining our observations to the Scots alone. For the present, then, let a single parenthetical remark suffice—namely, that it is our matured conviction, after having perused, we may almost say, every scrap extant bearing upon the discussion, that, notwithstanding the endless volumes which have been written, the more minute and interesting facts of the case have yet to be evoked. Nay, more ; we do not hesitate to say, that the most recent investigator of this complicated and somewhat mysterious topic, Dr Latham, is—always excepting John Pinkerton— farthest from the truth, since he expresses his belief, on most frivolous and untenable grounds, that ' the Picts *may* have been Scandinavians.' "

In the " London Quarterly Review," No. IV. for September 1854, another article by Mr Rhind occurs as a Review of Worsaae's "Account of the Danes and Norwegians in England, Scotland, and Ireland." This paper furnishes us with Mr Rhind's opinion of the nature and amount of the Norse influence in Britain, and especially in Scotland, and was noted as remarkable at the time of its appearance, by competent judges, who only came to know of its authorship in after days.

The first decided symptom of pulmonary disease in Mr Rhind was manifested in the autumn of 1853, and his health now required him to select warmer quarters for the winter than his own northern home could furnish. Up to this time he had been able for considerable bodily exertion. He enjoyed shooting and boating, and took part in the exploration of ancient remains. The immediate change in his physical power is expressed in a letter to his friend Dr Davis, written from Clifton in April 1854.—"The ascent of a gentle acclivity has now more terrors for me than climbing to a point in the Mont Blanc range 10,000 feet above the sea-level had two or three years ago."

As his purpose was to proceed to the Scotch Bar, he meant to have attended the law classes at Edinburgh during the winter of 1853–4, but he had now to retreat to Clifton. Here he received accounts of the death of his elder and only surviving brother, and soon after he was led to abandon his design of studying for the bar. In a letter to me written from Clifton, on 7th November 1854, he refers to his interest in the prosperity of the Society. "I assure you I will do what I can to write something for the Antiquaries, for I am quite of your mind that it is a necessary duty to do so on the part of every one who professes to take an interest in national antiquities and in the Society, which, whatever its shortcomings, *must* be regarded as the representative of them, and must be upheld as such."

The winter of 1854–5 was partly spent at Ventnor, whence he frequently wrote to me, and from which he sent a paper printed in our "Proceedings," (vol. ii. p. 72) on the "Bronze Swords occasionally attributed to the Romans." In the course of the same season he prepared a paper on "British Primeval Antiquities; their Present Treatment and their Real Claims."

This paper after being read to the Society, was printed by Mr Rhind as a pamphlet for the public, its main object being to create a healthy reverence throughout the country for the remains of early times, and to secure their more careful treatment afterwards. With the same object he afterwards wrote a paper " On the Present Condition of the Monuments of Egypt and Nubia," which is printed in the " Archæological Journal " for 1856.

In announcing to me the completion of this paper on British Antiquities, he thus wrote of its purport (Ventnor, 9th February 1855)—

" It relates to the neglect and danger to which national primeval relics are exposed. For some time I have been inquiring into this subject, and have devoted to it a good deal of trouble, and shall have to expend still more, particularly in examining additional blue books and other parliamentary papers, which a friend in the House of Commons has promised to send me. At first I intended embodying my materials in the form of a review article, but I then thought that the subject was likely to receive much more attention if brought before a society, one of whose cardinal duties is to see after the interests of archæological remains. That being done, and the society (if it thought proper) being induced to take some active step, I would be disposed to go to the expense of printing the paper afterwards as a pamphlet for more general circulation, in the expectation that it might be productive of some good. I say this because, feeling convinced that the success of archæology depends upon the better conservation of antiquarian remains, I have already exerted myself in some degree to that end, and intend continuing to do so, in so far as it may be in my power. I am quite sure that you will feel with me in this matter."

In the year 1854, Mr Rhind wrote an article for the " Ulster Journal of Archæology," (vol. ii. p. 100) in which he recorded the " Results of Excavations in Sepulchral Cairns in the North of Scotland, Identical in Internal Design with the Great Chambered Tumuli on the Banks of the Boyne in Ireland." These excavations had been executed at various times under Mr Rhind's personal superintendence. From such investigations he always anticipated useful results, and at a later period he expressed his opinion on the general subject in the following terms :—

" But however valuable such repositories as those alluded to may be, and however important we may regard the aggregation of antiquarian relics, it should always be kept prominently in mind, that the field from which primeval archæology has most to hope for is the careful survey and excavation of early remains. To me it seems that the special encouragement, furtherance, and undertaking of such explorations, should be the prime function of bodies incorporated with a view to archæological study ; and particularly of that body in England whose position, means, and representative character at once warrant and demand exertion—the Society of Antiqnaries of London. Researches of this kind are peculiarly the work for associated energy and conjoined resources, which can best accomplish them extensively and systematically. They are also the essential pabulum, the necessary element of that scientific progress in ethnological inquiry, which alone imparts dignity, utility, and solid value to antiquarian pursuits ; and therefore, if societies existing for the interests of these should fail to direct a due proportion of their efforts to clear the way for an onward march, they may survive as centres of barren co-operation, but their tendency will be to sink into mere embodiments of elaborate triviality, retarding, as cumberers of the ground, the true advancement of the science which they would profess to have in charge."[1]

The following passages regarding the excavations in question, and some of the conclusions deducible from them, occur in a letter to Dr Davis, written from Clifton on the 2d June 1854 :—

" If health, however, permit me to carry on many of the excavations in the North which I project, I am not without hopes of securing some tolerable specimens [of Crania.] But this, as I have said, entirely depends, I regret, on the state of my health, for it is impossible, I have found, to carry on such researches satisfactorily without personal superintendence ; and such superintendence, when the object is in a remote district, involves considerable exertion and exposure.

" I certainly am disposed at present to regard the Cairns as *somewhat*

[1] British Archæology, its Progress and Demands. Preface, p. 8. Lond. 1858.

older than the "Picts' Houses," but not much so ; for, apart from other considerations, there is a degree of similarity in the method in which they have both been built, that I conceive marks them as being nearly synchronous (if I may so use the word). This similarity is more appreciable to one engaged in the excavation of them, than it could be made by description ; but it certainly exists, only the workmanship in the Cairns is somewhat ruder, and therefore, *perhaps*, of slightly more ancient date. Any such opinion, however, is liable to a little modification as facts accumulate ; but, reasoning from present grounds, I think it is not far wrong.

"When you ask the question, 'Must we not refer both (cairns and 'Picts' houses') to the Picts ?' I am certainly quite disposed to answer in the affirmative, with only one apparent *petitio principii* (which might, however, be made good), namely, that *those* remains belong, not to an Allophylian race, but to the earliest Celtic population of North Britain. I confess that this question is not at present perhaps capable of complete solution ; but assuming the fact to be as I have stated it, then I believe the memorials in question to be Pictish, because, after as minute an examination of the disputed subject as I am capable of instituting, I feel persuaded that the *northern* Picts (at least) were the descendants of the early Gael. But although this is my opinion, and I presume is yours, from your question, still it is not universal, as there are many who believe that the Picts were not Gael at all, but an invading Gothic people, who took possession of the territory they held about the Christian era, according to some, and a century or two later, according to others. Although all parties would probably agree that the remains in question are early Celtic (overlooking for the present the Allophylian theory), there would not necessarily be the same unanimity as to their being strictly Pictish ; but of all this, I dare say, you are well aware, and I only allude to the subject because you asked my opinion."

In March 1855, Mr Rhind submitted a statement to Lord Duncan, at that time the Scotch Lord of the Treasury, with the view of obtaining official directions that all primeval vestiges should be carefully laid down on the Ordnance map of Scotland, which would then "exhibit an additional phase of usefulness by furnishing, as it were, an easily-consulted index, of immense service in archæological inquiries, which would show at a glance where certain relics are located, or what remains exist in specific districts,—a species of information which at present is perfectly unattainable, except by minute and generally impracticable personal research."

It was to follow up this attempt, and very much in consequence of suggestions made to me by Mr Rhind, that the Society of Antiquaries resolved to bring the subject under the notice of the Michaelmas County meetings of this year all over Scotland, with the view of obtaining a general and influential expression of opinion in favour of the proposed addition to the objects of the Ordnance Survey. He took a warm and direct interest in forwarding this movement of the Society; and when he was in London in October 1855, on the point of starting for Egypt, he wrote to me :—

"I got the copies of the circular which you sent to me, as also three others from Mr Robertson ; and I communicated with friends who would see that a responsive resolution was proposed, and the matter ventilated in Ross, Caithness, Sutherland, Orkney, Berwick, Inverness, Perth, Kincardine, and one or two other shires. On my requesting the Kilkenny Society to adopt the same course with regard to the landowners of the south-east of Ireland, they readily agreed to do so ; and in England, too, I hope something by-and-by will be done, so that the movement may be general, and therefore more effective."

The winter of 1855–6 was spent in Egypt, in the course of which Mr Rhind began those researches in the Tombs at Thebes, which were to bear such remarkable fruits. I need hardly say that the numerous objects of interest, discovered by him at the cost of great labour and expense (including a set of bilingual papyri and a painted bier, both supposed to be unique), were all sent to our National Museum. In a letter, written to me from Thebes on 24th January 1856, the following passage occurs :—

"It is my earnest desire to add to our museum such a series of Egyptian antiquities as will form a fair comparative representation of the archæology of the extraordinary people who lay so near the primary fountains of civilisation. With this view, I shall gladly purchase where I can, objects suitable for my purpose, which any of the peasantry around may possess, with the view of supplementing where the results of my own excavations may be wanting."

However much engrossed Mr Rhind might be in his own special pursuits, he was at all times ready to take an interest in and to forward the researches of friends who applied to him for assistance.

Writing to Dr Davis, from Thebes, on 8th Feb. 1856, regarding his efforts to procure modern skulls for him in Egypt, he says :— " For this you may be very sure that I shall keep an outlook, as I hold it to be selfish, if one can help those at home, especially friends, to lose an opportunity of doing so, when they themselves may not easily have any other means of coming at what they want."

In the month of November 1856, Mr Rhind published a little volume entitled " Egypt ; its Climate, Character, and Resources as a Winter Resort."   Its object is thus stated in the preface :—

" I have been led to prepare this book, conceiving that the modest position which it assumes to occupy required to be filled up, and that it was almost a duty to attempt to do so.   Although I am not without hope that its contents may have some interest for those desirous only to increase their acquaintance with the realities of eastern travel, the whole design has acquired its colour from having been undertaken chiefly with a view to those who have to think of countries with reference to the sanative influence of their climates."

The volume contained not only the results of the author's experience, but also thermometrical notes contributed by Lord Haddo (late Earl of Aberdeen), Sir Gardener Wilkinson, and others.

Mr Rhind spent part of the summer of 1856 at Sibster, and in the course of it resumed the excavation of some of the remains in his neighbourhood.   The result was communicated to the Society in a paper entitled " Notes of Excavations of Tumuli in Caithness made in the summer of 1856 " printed in the " Proceedings," vol. ii. p. 372. In it he makes the following statements :—

" It is scarcely necessary to notice, in so cursory a manner, that these four tumuli, in the simplicity of the interments, without the not unusual accompaniments of primeval burials, find many coincidences, particularly in the north, and add to a large aggregate of facts of a like nature. A careful survey of these has for some time seemed to me an inquiry of decided importance, which would probably involve a necessity for material modification of the 'current classifications, and limit the applicability of the psychological deductions which have commonly attributed to primeval ages certain feelings on the subject of futurity, without sufficient reference to the special divergences indicated by observed data, which, to say the least, will hardly verify the exactness of such a universal scheme of primeval religion. I cannot obtrude this subject here, especially as I hope shortly to develop, in a more appropriate and extended form, some of the views to which a consideration of this matter is calculated to lead."

In July of this year a Congress of the Archæological Institute was held in Edinburgh. Mr Rhind took a warm interest in all the preliminary arrangements for it; and Mr Way assures me that his exertions largely contributed to its success.

At this meeting, Mr Rhind read a paper " On Megalithic Remains in Malta," which affords a specimen of his careful system of induction, and his cautious refusal to adopt conclusions from merely traditional premises. He also read a communication " On the History of Systematic Classification of Primeval Relics," in which he pointed out that the idea of arranging by fixed progressive periods had not originated with northern archæologists, but had been discussed in Scotland long before it took shape in Scandinavia. Both papers are printed in the " Archæological Journal " for 1856.

The winter of 1856-7 was again spent in Egypt, when Mr Rhind resumed the excavations among the tombs at Thebes which he had commenced in the previous season. In a letter to Dr Davis, from Goornch, Thebes, dated 9th January 1857, Mr Rhind thus describes his arrangements :—

" Having stated to our consul-general, Mr Bruce, when at Cairo, the objects I had in view, he very kindly applied for and obtained for me a firman from the viceroy. Armed with this precious document, under the seal of Said Pacha, enjoining all the governors throughout Egypt to aid me in whatever I may require, and permitting me to excavate wherever I like in the whole country, I possess here, where I have taken up my position, a sort of irresponsible power. I certainly shall not abuse it; and I do need it, for I have a shocking set of scoundrels to deal with. I have already forty men at work at one point and twenty at another. At the former I was cheered yesterday by the discovery of eight mummy cases, and to-day of six more. They were not within a tomb, but give evidence, I hope, of the proximity of one, and I shall diligently persevere in search of it, as, from the position, it would probably be interesting. On Monday I intend to have fifty more men in the valley of the splendid tombs of the kings. I have several times gone diligently over the ground, and I have marked off several spots that seem promising. . . . I have also originated an excavation on the Island of Elephantine, 150 miles up the river, which Lord Henry Scott and Mr Stobart have undertaken to superintend for me, sending for me should it promise favourably."

The exertions thus undergone by Mr Rhind seem to have been greater than his strength could bear; for in writing to Dr Davis from Palermo on 8th May 1857, he states :—

" In the early months of spring I was myself by no means so well as I could have wished, partly I believe in consequence of over exertion, which it was difficult for the time to avoid. This compelled me to relinquish some of my designs, and one in particular, which I greatly regret, a series of excavations, in what we call the Western Valley, which, from its remote situation, would have involved an amount of fatigue to reach it daily on horseback for the purpose of supervision, that after a very unmistakeable warning I did not dare to think of undertaking. I kept to work vigorously however at various points nearer home, and at one of these in particular I met with very considerable success. My reward there was a large and remarkable tomb with its deposit in untouched security."

In this letter, Mr Rhind adds :—

" After leaving Thebes I had intended pitching my tent for another month, as last year, in the shadow of the Pyramids of Geezeh, but I found that the season was rather far advanced. Accordingly I sailed from Alexandria on the 4th of April for Malta, and thence here, where I have now been established for more than a fortnight enjoying myself thoroughly. A more delicious place I have never seen. The eye may be almost constantly intoxicated with the exquisite landscape ; and all around the city the air is redolent of the perfumes of endless varieties of flowers, orange blossoms, and the other products of a most luxuriant vegetation. Man is the sole saddening element in the prospect, both from what he too often appears to be in point of comfort, and from what we know he *is* in point of liberty. It had been my design to go on to Naples and Rome, but every thing here is so attractive that I shall not tear myself away until it is necessary to turn homewards."

The summer of 1857 was partly spent at Sibster, from which place he wrote to me on 14th September, a letter, containing the following interesting remarks on the Round Towers or Burghs which are peculiar to the Northern Parts of Scotland.

" I shall answer your last question [about burghs] first, as to whether I have bestowed much attention on the subject. Whenever and wherever I could, I have not failed to note everything that came in my way respecting the burghs, and I have also made them a subject of special inquiry. I know a large number of facts connected with them, but I do not feel in a condition to hazard as yet definite results. I have never been able to hear of any of these peculiar memorials except in the northern division of Scotland, the Orkney, Shetland, and Western Isles; and I have made it a matter of very wide search in the antiquarian topographical literature of England and Ireland to find some trace of them and of the allied ' Picts' houses,' of which I have been disposed to regard them as the outgrowth or development. I have never been able to find any definite allusion to their existence in Ireland, although *I have particularly looked for such, because I saw reason to expect that they might be in that country* for the following reason. We have in Scotland a remarkable class of chambered cairns. In the north I have been a great deal among these and Picts' houses, and I have been led to perceive in the structural portions of both a certain conformity which I could not exactly make clear to you in a short note, but which would warrant a belief that both were the products of the same architectural development. The burgh, if I am right in what I have said, would follow the same analogy. Now I have inquired in vain as yet for either a Pict's house or a burgh in Ireland ; *but chambered cairns like ours are there*, such as those at New Grange, and one in Kilkenny, although I cannot make out that they are very numerous.   Still their presence has to me always induced the expectation of at least the correlative Pict's house being at some time discovered.   If the towers Dr Simpson has seen are identical with Dundornadilla, I hope he has taken a note of their structure and locality.   If they are merely circular buildings, without possessing the double concentric walls, they will still be interesting, but I do not think they would be burghs.   In answer to your question, I would say that this is the distinguishing mark of the burgh.   Simple circular buildings may be found in any country, and are perhaps not uncommon products of early mediæval architecture ; but even were such structures found in Scotland, which I do not know, or at the moment remember, I should require to be well assured of their *archaic uncemented* construction, and to judge somewhat from their position before classifying them as burghs."

On 8th October 1857, he wrote Dr Davis from Edinburgh—

' I am delighted to see that your cranial treasures have attained such valuable extent ; and when you allude to what I have been able to do to swell them, you estimate much more highly than I do the little aid it has been in my power to give.   Most gladly would I ere now have put you in possession of some specimens to supply your deficiency of modern Celtic types, but I have hitherto been completely baffled. . . . . I have no reasonable doubt, however, that were I ever to be restored to a degree of health, which I cannot conceal from myself it would be too sanguine to expect, such as would enable me to undertake researches in the northern counties of the extent which I earnestly desire, then, being personally present in Highland localities, I might confidently hope to procure at the same time what you so much desire.   Sometimes recollections of this kind tempt me to be querulous and repining, but I should not forget that with much to bemoan I have much to be thankful for."

A few days after this letter was written, Mr Rhind was prostrated by an unexpected attack of illness, which confined him for a long time, and reduced him to such a state of weakness, that although Dr Davis, who had come to Scotland on a tour, was in the same hotel with him in Edinburgh, he was unable to see him.   Writing to Dr Davis from Malaga, on 11th December 1857, he thus describes his illness :—

" The attack of hæmoptysis which prostrated me in Edinburgh was most unexpected, and very considerable. I was just about going out to church on the morning of the Indian fast-day, when, without any apparent proximate cause that I could remember, except it were bending a little before, I felt blood flow into my chest, and I lost perhaps a tea-cupful. . . . . . . I have now been settled down for a fortnight, and the change has already done me a world of good. I have gained strength ; appetite become vigorous ; chest sensations apparently subsiding into their former character. . . . . . . After two winters spent in Egypt, I do not as yet find this an unsatisfactory change for the climate of the Nile. It is several degrees cooler certainly, probably 9 or 10 in the middle of the day, but is still sufficiently warm for any one who would be content with the sunniest days of our own August."

At the Anniversary Meeting of the Society, on St Andrew's Day 1857, Mr Rhind was elected an Honorary Member.

While at Malaga, in the spring of 1858, Mr Rhind heard of his father's death, an event which was thus communicated to Dr Davis in a letter from Algiers, written on the 26th March of this year :—

" Early in February I had a great grief, in the intelligence (until quite previously), entirely unexpected, of the death of a most affectionate father, whose whole being was devoted to me. The affliction was the more severe, that the stroke, by snapping the last tie of near relationship, leaves me as it were alone. Feeling that a change from a place saddened by so gloomy an association would be desirable, we left Malaga about the middle of this month, and crossed over to Algeria."

To those acquainted with Mr Rhind's warm, loving nature, the depth of such a wound may be estimated. Some of the thoughts which sustained him under his feelings of desolation, we may gather from the following verses, which I find copied into one of his commonplace books :—

"WHO IS ALONE?[1]

How heavily the path of life
Is trod by him who walks alone ;
Who hears not on his dreary way
Affection's sweet and cheering tone ;

[1] Hymns and Poems for the Sick and Suffering, p. 136.

> Aloue although his heart should bound
> With love to all things great and fair,
> They love not him,—there is not one
> His sorrow or his joy to share.
>
> *   *   *   *   *
>
> Who is alone, if God be nigh ?
> Who shall repine at loss of friends,
> While he has One of boundless power,
> Whose constant kindness never ends ?—
> Whose presence felt enhances joy,
> Whose love can stop each flowing tear,
> And cause, upon the darkest cloud,
> The pledge of mercy to appear."

In the letter to Dr Davis last quoted, Mr Rhind thus refers to the question of Treasure Trove, in the adjustment of which he felt great interest :—

" Before the last occurrence diverted my thoughts, and when, in point of strength, I had so far recovered as to be able to undertake a little work, I prepared what I had for some time promised, an Exposition of the Law of Treasure Trove for the Scottish Antiquaries."

This paper was read to the Society, and is noticed in the Proceedings (vol. iii. p. 76). It was printed as a pamphlet, with a preface, dated Malaga, 15th January 1858, under the title of " The Law of Treasure Trove—How can it be best adapted to accomplish useful results ?"

In a letter to me from Algiers, dated 30th March 1858, he thus writes of his new quarters :—

" I need not say I have very great satisfaction in noting any particulars that may be of use to our friend Innes, as regards spring quarters. For myself, I have been very greatly pleased with this place, in point of climate, since I have been here. The air is singularly soft and balmy, without, however, being humid or relaxing ; and as March and April have the reputation of being normally of this character here, I do not know any place where these months could be spent more agreeably. As to earlier spring and winter, there is a certain proportion of rain and changeable weather, as everywhere on the Mediterranean seaboard, but less, so far as I can judge, than at any point on the northern shores, excepting only Malaga. By the end of April or early in May, the heat, although, it is said, not oppressive, becomes so considerable as to indicate removal to those who, contemplating spending the summer in our home climate, do not wish to accustom themselves to a high temperature. By the way, one thing is probably worth mentioning, that local medical opinion seems to be, that the air here being somewhat stimulant, does not always suit those who are nervously excitable, and has a tendency to arouse irritation in that direction.

" In point of other attractions, the country around Algiers is of its kind the most beautiful I ever saw—ravines and slopes, infinitely diversified by the most luxuriant vegetation. These, too, are in all directions penetrated by excellent roads, and so the drives and points of view are very various.

" The town itself is bustling and lively—too much so to my taste. The hotels are good, and their scale of charges about the same as usually prevails in France. For a strong man there are plenty of expeditions on all sides by steamer or diligence, and much, if not always of special, of adequate interest to see, in Roman sites, the outline of the country, the Kabyles, and so on. If Innes thinks of coming here this season, and conceives there is anything I can do for him beforehand, I shall have the greatest pleasure in being of any use to him."

In the beginning of May, Mr Rhind left Algiers for the south of France, where he lingered for some weeks, Avignon being his head quarters. Part of the summer and autumn was spent at Sibster. On 23d August 1858, he writes to Dr Davis from this place " a hurried line respecting the Sutherland (Dunrobin) skull as you wish it," in which he recapitulates his reasons, formerly stated to myself, for believing the deposit to be Scandinavian :—

" 1. The sculptured stones (of which one was used as a cap-stone) being native and peculiar, were not likely to be regarded by roving strangers, who were inimical also to the indigenous population ; and they (the Norsemen) might naturally make use of a convenient slab.

" 2. The situation not far from the shore gives probability to a Scandinavian origin.

" 3. The grave, in its structure of slab-stones and general character, corresponds with an interment which I knew in Caithness, of undoubted Norse origin, as the usual two shell-shaped brooches were present.

" 4. The grave seemed to indicate a date almost, if not quite, contemporaneous with the native use of the sculptured stones ; and so a native population would hardly use one for an uncontemplated purpose.

" I think the objection to your line of argument would be—(1) The difficulty of drawing too strict a line between the symbols on the pre-Christian and the Christian stones ; (2) and chiefly, The Norsemen are much more likely to have buried in this fashion as pagans, and not as Christians. Their paganism in the North of Scotland is of much later date by several centuries than the introduction of Christianity among the native tribes. Add to which this deposit is *prima facie* (though not necessarily) pagan, as it had at least one accompaniment, a corroded (apparently) ferrule of iron for the haft, perhaps of spear or pike."

In September, Mr Rhind came southwards. I was not in Edinburgh when he passed through, but he wrote to me afterwards of his endeavours to assist Mr Hamilton, to whom was entrusted the construction of the cases for the National Museum, by giving him all the facts suggested by his experience, and by introducing him to the officers of the British Museum, who were most conversant with the subject. In October, Mr Rhind took up his quarters at Hyeres in the South of France, from which he wrote to me, on 28th October—

" I am here establishing myself rather nearer home than usual—at all events, for the winter—with the intention of moving down the Spanish coast, or into Italy, in January, when the harsh spring winds may be anticipated. At a first start, I am quite charmed with this place. The views are exquisite ; the vegetation almost richer than Italian ; the hotel where I am staying exceedingly comfortable ; and the climate, it is to be hoped, enjoyable."

In this letter he recurs to the subject of Treasure Trove, to the settlement of which he wished to give a fresh impulse, and adds,— " The time was thought opportune to bring together the two pamphlets on British Antiquities and Treasure Trove, and I have set them out in a volume with a new preface, the sentiments of which

I hope you will approve." This preface, from which I have already quoted (p. 9), is dated from Clifton, 12th October 1858.

In a letter to Dr Davis, written from Hyeres on 26th December 1858, he says:—

" I am much pleased to have your opinion of the photograph of the Maltese skull. Your attribution of it to an African type coincides with that of certain Italian physicists, Orioli of Bologna, being, I think, one. Its history is this,—It was found with crumbling bones in a species of crypt, in the Megalithic remains at Hagar Kim, in Malta,—a paper on which I read at the Congress of the Archæological Institute at Edinburgh in 1856. The specialties of these curious vestiges, and generally the primeval archæology of the Mediterranean coasts and islands, offers a somewhat important field of research, which I always try to keep in view. I am just now finishing a long paper of about sixty MS. pages on one branch of the subject, 'Megalithic Vestiges in North Africa and their place in Primeval Archæology.' "

The paper just referred to is printed in "Archæologia, vol. xxxviii. p. 252.

In the beginning of February 1859, Mr Rhind left Hyeres for Nice, whence he proceeded by Genoa and Leghorn to Rome, which he reached just before the commencement of the Carnival. Writing to me from Rome on 2d March, he says:—

" I need not tell you of the Archæological profusion here. It is over-powering in quantity and dazzling in kind. During the past week I have examined most of the ruins of ancient Rome. The art galleries and the churches I have not yet entered upon. With regard to these, however, I intend, on this occasion, only to familiarize myself with the most prominent exemplars ; and my time I propose chiefly to devote to the study of the Etruscan antiquities, with respect to which, I want to lay a good basement in my memory for comparative purposes."

Leaving Rome on the last day of March, Mr Rhind spent a few days in Naples, and then feeling the need of repose after the excitement of sight-seeing, took up his abode for some weeks in the beautiful Island of Capri. " The change," he writes to Dr Davis,

" was most pleasant and useful, allowing an opportunity for digest-
ing, so to say, the crowded impressions of two tolerably laborious
months."

The revolutionary events then occurring in that country compelled
Mr Rhind to alter his plans and led him to hasten his return to
England without visiting the Balearic Islands, which he was
" anxious to see for the sake of their curious remains—the Talyots."
On his return he resumed his residence at Clifton.

At this time a Committee of our Society was engaged in determining the principles on which the arrangement of the National
Museum was to proceed. Mr Rhind, as I have said, had at various
times visited, and carefully examined, the chief Museums of Antiquities in Europe. He had done this with a definite object and
purpose, and as I was naturally desirous of obtaining the result of
his experience at the time when we were about to fix the future
arrangement of our own collection, he was so good as embody his
views in the following " Memorandum on the Arrangement of the
National Museum of Scottish Antiquities " :—

" With regard to the classification of an Archæological Museum such as
ours, there are, I think, at least two points which may form an axiomatic
basis to start from.

" The first is, that a collection calculated to teach inductively or deduc-
tively, should be arranged with respect to its instructive capabilities, and
not merely in the manner most convenient for generic adjustment or
reference, as for example books in a library.

" The second is, that such a collection being the embodiment, or rather
the data, of scientific inquiries not fully developed, speculative, and progressive, should not, as far as possible, be classified according to any
conclusion that may be doubtful, and thus cramped into a mere illustration of a foregone formula, instead of being allowed, by a quasi-natural
juxta-position of the objects, to evolve whatever shades of meaning they
may bear.

" If these be the essentials of classification which we should endeavour
to approach, we must fail to approve of either of the two systems with

which (as adopted on a large scale) we are familiar. The one is that embraced by the Royal Irish Academy, which may be called what I have termed a mere generic adjustment, whereby, in consequence of arrangement, simply according to material (wood, bone, stone, &c.) which may belong to any age, race or country, the function of teaching is almost altogether abrogated, and what little precise knowledge has been hardly won of primeval ages, is nearly enwrapped in its original chaos. The other is the method of the three processional periods which is commonly described as Danish, which is in use at Copenhagen, at Schwerin, under Herr Lisch, who, I believe, first employed it, and not to mention other collections, is practically the plan followed in the British room of the British Museum. To it arises the objection under the second head, that its teaching is not unequivocal, and is admitted by native investigators themselves not to be of universal application, even in the three Scandinavian countries where it is most strongly maintained, while, with regard to Britain, the sum of our experience up to this point will not at all warrant such unqualified precision.

"Further, in both the systems there is the radical defect, that either, if rigidly carried out, involves the dismemberment of sepulchral deposits or other finds, which, it being one of the peculiarities in Britain, consist often of objects of diverse material, and which, precisely for this reason, constitute in their integrity our most valuable data.

"On these grounds, I conceive that a blending of the two systems, or rather following an arrangement springing naturally from the relics themselves, and, above all, from the circumstances in which they have been found, would be at once more scientifically just and practically useful. In such arrangement, I would admit but one inevitable generalization, even that to be confronted by a scheme of constant correctives of simple application. This generalization would merely be a recognition of the relative inferiority and superiority of artistic appliances and products, a gradation inferentially related to the lapse of time—as the broad teaching of history and experience is progress in those matters—but a gradation not necessarily chronometrical, and the precise significance of which it would be the object of this corrective system gradually to unfold, rather than preliminarily to assume.

"A short outline of the practical details I should propose to follow will be more explanatory than an exposition of abstract principles.

"Supposing the classification were to be commenced as you enter the Museum, I should begin by arranging in the first wall case to the right, all the stone weapons and implements now in our possession, not forming part of heterogeneous finds. In the same case I would place those urns, pateræ and ornaments, &c., of a similarly isolated character, the like of which, experience or analogy may teach us, has been found in conjunction with stone relics in this country. In a portion of this case duly defined, and headed " Illustrative," as opposed to " Native," I should exhibit corresponding objects from other countries, including Irish relics ; but not English relics, which, for obvious ethnographical reasons, it would not at this stage be necessary to dissociate from Scottish. In continuation of this case, I would have a space for early mixed and indeterminate objects, and then proceed on the same plan with the metallic and correlative relics, taking care, as before, to be guided, if possible, by facts, or at all events, by analogy and judgment, in determining what vestiges are to be associated.

"Then, as to the practical commentary on this stringing together or quasi-classification of what may be called the waifs or separate objects, I would have in the wall cases immediately opposite, or in some instances in cases on the floor, any group in its integrity which constituted any one sepulchral deposit, or the contents of any one primeval dwelling ; a description of archæological material of great value, and not unlikely to accumulate from the increasing care of excavators. Already we have several. Accompanying these, I would have, whenever drawings exist, illustrations of the remains, and even positions in which they were discovered—representations which might be merely the engravings in use—to illustrate descriptive papers, original sketches, or photographic copies of these on a small scale, now so easily and cheaply produced. Models also of the vestiges which have yielded the relics, and, indeed, of all others of a corresponding character, are also a species of treasure which should find their place here, and the accumulation of which ought to receive every attention : nor would I limit this mode of illustration to the groups. In every instance, where similar material exists for the elucidation of what I have termed the isolated objects, in the opposite wall-cases, I would likewise back *them* with such exponents of their history. For both the groups and the separate objects, I would also have another common rule—that each should bear a plainly legible statement of at least the place and description of monument in which it was found, along with a precise reference to volume and page of the " original source," whenever the circumstances under which it was discovered have been recorded, whether in MS. in the archives of the Society, or in print in the Society's Proceedings, or elsewhere.

" It is thus by blending and reflecting, one against the other, the intimations of single objects—relics in their primitive groups, and monuments, all in their mutual co-relation,—that we shall best extract their fullest signification, and at the same time guard against going beyond it.

" As I have here chiefly to deal with pre-historic vestiges, I need hardly go farther, and it is unnecessary to add, that at the conclusion of a sequence such as the foregoing notes indicate, we should come to works bearing evidence of direct Roman influence. Of a later period still, we have as yet in Scotland recovered very few relics corresponding in date to the Anglo-Saxon antiquities so numerous in England, and this, in fact, is one of the dimmest vistas in Scottish archæology. At the outskirts, and at the close of this epoch, we come to Scoto-Irish products—the contents of a few Scandinavian graves on our coasts, distinguished generally by their shell-shaped brooches, and hordes like the valuable addition from Orkney which the Museum has lately received. Then antiquarian inquiry, already begun to find outlet in other paths, is bereft almost entirely of much of its older field, and its materials and products, at once more full and more precise, fall readily, with only occasional difficulties, into chronological line.

" I have thus hurriedly endeavoured to sketch the general features of the conception I have formed of a scientific archæological collection. After acquaintance with nearly all the museums in Europe, the impression which remains with me is, that the foregoing outline represents the idea of what one would wish a National assemblage of relics to be, as a medium whereby to arrive readily, practically, and in an unbiassed shape, at an estimate of the archæological characteristics of any given country. It need scarcely be added that such an arrangement implies neither particular difficulty nor undue extravagance of space. It would require care and judgment, but no more trouble than such an object legitimately demands ; and in its minuter developments such as the supplying of titles, illustrations, and references, the work could be gradually completed not necessarily before but after the Museum is opened."

A. HENRY RHIND.

CLIFTON, 11th June 1859.

In the month of July 1859, Mr Rhind came to Edinburgh, where he resided during that month and part of August. In the end of July he attended the meeting of the Archæological Institute at Carlisle where I met him. He only remained for a couple of days, and feeling unable for the fatigue of country excursions, he confined himself to an examination of the local museum of the Institute, and to attendance in the Sections at the reading of the more remarkable papers.

At a later period of the season he arranged for a lease of the beautiful mansion of Down House near Bristol, of which, on 10th October, he thus wrote to me at Malvern, where I was at the time—

" I have been getting settled in my new abode, into which I moved a week ago. Although I am pretty well accustomed to moving my tent, yet it is a sad tax on time and other occupations shaking into place, when the result promises to be something like permanency. When it is over, however, and my *penates* are fixed, I fancy I may count upon having no other flitting in the full sense of the term until the last."

He was at the same time meditating his usual winter flight, but amid all his distractions, he kept in view the arrangement of the Museum at Edinburgh. In the same letter he writes me—

" I have heard from Mr M'Culloch [the keeper of the Museum] several times, and I write as fully as I can in answer to his questions. You know, however, the difficulty of realising the positions of absent things, and of tracing in and by letters, transpositions which a glance might set at rest. So far as I make out he has been getting on nicely; but when you get home, do look in and keep him, as far as possible, to principles, which, with the best will in the world, one is apt to overlook in a natural, and, indeed, so far commendable anxiety to arrange for the eye and for facility of cataloguing."

It was Mr Rhind's wish to have been present at the meeting of the British Association which took place at Aberdeen in September of this year: he took especial interest in the proceedings of the Ethnological Section, and the relative Archæological Museum formed under the auspices of Mr Charles E. Dalrymple and other members of a local committee. But as he afterwards wrote to Dr Davis from Boulogne on 7th November, he was unable to enjoy the pleasure : " To me it was a decided privation to have been obliged to forego the meeting at Aberdeen, as besides the other inducements, I had counted upon meeting so many friends together who are not easily brought within reach otherwise." In this letter he informed Dr Davis that he had been detained at Boulogne from the effects of a bad cold caught during the passage across, which proved unexpectedly boisterous, by exposure from which he could find no shelter, in consequence of the crowd on board and the miserably uncomfortable construction of the steamer. He however felt so much better as to propose to begin his journey to Hyeres on the following day. On that day, however, he had a recurrence of his old complaint, which completely prostrated him, and detained him at Boulogne for a month before he gathered even a feeble amount of strength. "You will readily believe," he afterwards wrote to Dr Davis from Hyeres on 3d March 1860, "that under these circumstances a journey across France in mid winter was rather an undertaking, but there was nothing else to be done, and by care and arrangement I accomplished it without detriment." In the same letter he writes—

"I have no doubt you have read Darwin's remarkable book on the "Origin of Species." I had it sent here with a parcel of others, and have just finished it. Viewed antagonistically or not, it is a great performance, from the evident and continuous thought with which it has been elaborated, and the free range which it evinces over a vast area of facts. Without as yet having been able to give it full consideration, I am disposed to think that he has done more than has ever been done formerly to show cause for believing that species are not necessarily fixed elemental points. But how far, and to what extent, the power and principle of mutability has been operative, is the question. Whether an inflexible logic, from specials to the widest generals, is to bear down all before it ; and whether an analogy, not necessarily of universal application, must be held to swamp all difficulties, is the issue. I should like to see this phase discussed by the professed physiologists and zoologists ; and I dare say this will come presently, but hitherto they seem to have been rather holding aloof."

In a letter to me from Hyeres, dated 27th February of this year, are the following passages on " The Picts," and " The Sculptured Stones of Scotland," which are well worth preserving :—

" As to the special point you mention, defining Galloway in the *tenth* century *Terra Pictorum*, I do not, like you, remember any authority applicable, otherwise than inferentially. But with regard to the actual ethnologic position of the Celtic population which we seem to find there later, *that* could only be dealt with as part of the general question affecting the Picts. And first of all, what force is to be given to the name Pict ? If we are to use it merely in a political sense (so to say) as describing the nation we find in East and North East Scotland, then it would have no more ethnographic significance than for example the terms Mercian or East Anglian in South Britain, and would fail to be a palpable distinction. But if we are to make it a test of race, and of generic import, we have the old problem in all its complexity. I myself greatly doubt the accuracy of a rigid application. I am satisfied as to the generic Kelticism of the Picts, but not that they were exclusively or specially Gælic, or specially Cymric. While, then, Bede lays down their boundaries to the South expressly enough, in his day, *as a nation*, we must not necessarily *ipso facto* conclude that the RACE *element* of *Pictism* was at all times, or at any time, restricted to the north of his line, and to the exclusion of Ireland—where, the more I used to think of it, the more I was convinced that there was not an uniformity in its Keltism. I should greatly like to see developed the line of inquiry which you point to, and which the new glimpses of Pictish institutions have opened up—namely, a minute comparison with the state of matters in Ireland and South Britain.

" As to the *Stones*, a section of what you mention is very much what I have been endeavouring to keep in view. With reference to a general idea, in demanding which you rather drive me into a corner, I would be disposed to formulate it somewhat thus :—

" 1. The crude figures in their simplicity (those we term symbols) have not hitherto been met with—at all events similarly grouped elsewhere.

" 2. The *ornamentation*,—interlaced knot work, and such like—was common in Roman work, particularly of late time.

" 3. Certain of the figures, such as some of the men and horses, have a strong resemblance to debased Roman work. To give one or two analogies :—on the fronts of Christian sarcophagi from the catacombs at Rome, and in incidental bas reliefs often merely built into modern walls in Italy, I have noted groups of considerable correspondence with the best of ours; such as men with kilt-like tunics, horses of the same full, rounded contour, ridden by men without stirrups and with pointed toes, a chariot with occupants like one at Meigle.

"As to the first (the symbols) I should not feel quite warranted to speculate whence they originated, although, judging by analogy and by *the epoch to which they seem referrible*, I should suspect that they sprung from some untraceable foreign germs, rather than consider that they were of pure native creation. But that they were a specially native *development* seems clear from their number and local restriction. The second and third, again, I should be inclined to look upon as almost entirely adopted and imitative products. If this view be correct, it should exercise an influence on what may be termed the archæological reading of the third (the figures, &c.), by making it doubtful whether they are intended to represent the contemporary dress or customs of the country.

"On the general ethnical questions hinging on the positive or negative affirmation of an early native art-growth, I could not here enter.

"I am now in correspondence with Italy on the subject of some of those reliefs and sarcophagi to which I alluded; but it is difficult to accomplish exactly what one wants. In a fortnight or so a friend of mine is going there, and I think I may be able to get some help through him. If you chance to have any spare copies of individual stones on thin paper, and would send me three, being of examples typically representative of respectively the symbols, the ornamenting knot-work, and the pictorial figures, they might be very useful in enabling me to send clear instructions by my friend."

In his next letter to me, dated 4th April, he writes :—

"Your letter, and the packet with the lithographs of the stones which you so practically replied to me by sending, arrived safely a fortnight ago, and I lost no time in employing the latter in the manner I had in view. I have not yet heard from Rome as to the results of the instructions I gave for a draughtsman's work, nor, indeed, do I expect to do so for some little time.

"The report of your last meeting shows a most thriving state of things. Accurate drawings and descriptions, like that by Captain Thomas of the houses in Harris, are of the highest interest, and I echo your wish that they (particularly the plans and drawings) were more numerous. I am very glad to be able to send you with this, I suppose in time for your next meeting, a paper, the materials for which have at various times cost

me much trouble in the gathering.   It forms part of the diggings in the
general archæology of the Old World, which I try to keep following out,
without being very hopeful, I am sad to confess it, that I shall ever be
able to complete my scheme."

The paper thus referred to was " On the Use of Bronze and Iron
in Ancient Egypt, with reference to General Archæology."   An
abstract of it is printed in our Proceedings, vol. iii. p. 464.

About the middle of April Mr Rhind began his homeward journey,
making Nismes his headquarters for two or three weeks, " as there
is a good deal of antiquarian interest there, and close by at Arles,"
reaching England early in June.   On the 15th of this month he
wrote Dr Davis on the subject of a series of ethnological queries,
which that gentleman proposed to put into the hands of competent
observers in different localities :—

" In the matter of the ' queries,' of course, I shall be most glad to be of
any use to you ; but when you and Stuart talk of my *opinion* on the subject as being of any value, I am only certain that you both very decidedly
overestimate it.   I think the form of the questions is well calculated to
get at the facts you want ; but I frankly confess to you that I should put
little or no reliance for purposes of sound deduction, upon the answers in
the mass which you are likely to receive.   Nobody will know better than
yourself how rare is the capacity for scientific observation, even in matters
where direct tangible testimony is alone involved, without the necessity of
the exercise of judgment.   But in the case of your queries, where the observer has to state general results (as in 2, 3, and 6), from a comparative
discrimination of many (say twenty) diverse units, I think the task is one
which, if well executed, would itself require a judicious and rational ethno-
loger.   Again, supposing that individual observers were tolerably capable,
there would almost necessarily be sufficient difference in their respective
mental processes of weighing evidence, to make the aggregate product an
accretion of *ununiform* items.   In fact, it seems to me that a series of
observations, such as those in question, to be of full practical value, would
require to be made by one practised eye, guided by one standard of elimination—in short, it is an affair in which, from the delicacy of the process,
as applied to minute ethnology, everything depends on the observer and
his judicial ability.   I would strongly, therefore, incline to the view that,

if you contemplate founding on a series of inquiries of the nature indicated in the 'queries,' it would be a very great matter if you could, in your own person, make the few local inspections that would be needed. Previously selecting your points, and provided with introductions, a tour of four or six weeks would, I believe, accomplish the work satisfactorily, and in such a manner that, if you came to build, you could rely upon the bricks."

In the month of August 1860 I had the pleasure of visiting Mr Rhind at his residence near Bristol. He was then busy with his book on Thebes, and in such health as enabled him to enjoy the society of his friends, and to take daily drives in his carriage. The season, however, was on the whole wet and gloomy, and he, in company with his friend Mr Palmer, who had been his companion at Hyeres, sailed for Madeira in the month of October.

While at Madeira he executed his settlements on the 1st January 1861.

Writing to Mr Earle from Madeira, on 10th April 1861, he says—

"I have got on exceedingly well through the whole season—at least keeping my ground, and working with some degree of steadiness. My Egyptian volume is now almost quite done ; and when I reach England, I hope, after a good revisal, to be ready to go to press. The only thing I feel sure about it is, that it will not to anybody, or intrinsically, represent the amount of labour it has cost me. We are looking forward to flight, and have arranged the mode. At one time our plan was to make for the Canary Islands, and thence by the coast of Africa to the south of Spain ; but a hitch as to the steamboats has obliged us to give up this on the present occasion, although I do so reluctantly, as I am anxious to learn something of the Guanche antiquities at Teneriffe. We have now fixed to sail direct to England about the 18th of May ; and before the end of that month I hope to be at home, where I shall speedily expect to welcome you, to get the light of your countenance, and the benefit of your experience, as to the killed shrubs, before going to see the results of your labours in your own vineyard."

In the end of May he reached his residence at Down House, where he spent the summer. In the beginning of September Mr Palmer came to visit him with the view of concerting plans for again spending the ensuing winter together in a warmer climate. On the second day after his arrival Mr Palmer was unexpectedly seized by hæmorrhage of the lungs. Writing to Mr Earle on the 11th Sept., Mr Rhind says—

"Alas! alas! there is anything in view but a visit to you this week. Poor Palmer came to me this day week looking wretchedly ill; and the night after but one he appeared at my bedside (at half-past two in the morning) coughing violently from hæmorrhage, and begging for help. Happily I had the needful appliances at hand. I got him to bed, and sat with him until we got a surgeon, before whose arrival the bleeding ceased."

Mr Palmer's death was thus announced to Mr Earle on the 20th September :—"My last letter would prepare you for our poor friend's illness taking the worst turn. And so it has been. He went calmly to his rest yesterday morning."

Mr Rhind again returned to Madeira for the winter of 1862. He thus writes to Mr Earle on 3d January 1862—

"I have settled down into the kind of fossil life which I followed (and which the nature of the place compels one to follow) last year. I am occupying the same rooms, meeting very many of the same people, revolving in my morning rides in the same narrow circles, which the bounding hills prescribe, and altogether feeling as if I had never left the island. There is a lamentable want of variety and life in this exile—that is undeniable. Indoors, of course, one has one's occupations; but the want of interesting objects, and, to some extent, of interesting people outside, makes what ought to be the pleasantest part of the day, often the least so. In the house in which I am staying, and which has some seventeen guests, we are, as to *personnel*, in some respects worse, in some respects better off, than last year. Of course the larger number of the people are simply of negative characteristics; and if we have none who are actually treasures, neither have we any—and it is something to say of a miscellaneous household—that are positively obnoxious. One-half are Germans; and as I have a general liking for their race, I am glad of the *interim*, and live.

" Two of our set are very good specimens in various ways ; but being Northerns (Sleswig men), and rather out of the way of the literary activity of Germany, they are not such ' full men'—to use Bacon's phrase—as their countrymen of corresponding position and education sometimes are." " I am looking forward with some degree of pleasure to my spring move. My plan is to sail for Teneriffe at the first of April, to spend three weeks or a month there, looking up the Guanche antiquities ; and then to make for Seville, by way of Cadiz, at the beginning of May. I should hope to spend a month pleasantly in and about Seville, and then to return to England, either by Lisbon or Gibraltar."

About six weeks later in the season (15th February) Mr Rhind wrote to me from Madeira. The following passage in his letter shows how he kindled up at any plan for elucidating native antiquities :—

" I saw in an Aberdeen paper, which was sent to me by the last mail, a report of your Spalding Club meeting. The account of what had been accomplished, and what was contemplated, seemed very satisfactory. The plan which you seem yet to keep partly in abeyance, I think is well worthy of every consideration—I mean following up the Sculptured Stones by a somewhat similar exemplification of the historical architecture of the north-east of Scotland. There never is likely to be such an opportunity as that offered by the united effort of a Club like the Spalding, for constructing a *corpus* of the historico-ethnographical materials of the northern counties—a work which, as well as appealing to our national feelings, must have a somewhat unexpected scientific value, from the evidence to be afforded as to the character of development in a comparatively isolated region. The mediaeval chartulary, and similar social illustrations, are one part of such a *corpus* ; the sculptured stones notably another ; the household, castellated, and ecclesiastical architecture would be another ; and I have for some time thought of suggesting to you one more, and yet an earlier link, to be taken up when the sculptured stones were finished, and illustrated by the same process of collocation and embodiment of thoroughly trustworthy facts and illustrations. What I mean is, a series of representations of a large number of the prominent and typical early vestiges of the northern counties—the hill forts, the circles and other ortholithic erections, the circle houses and Picts' Houses, the cairns and barrows, and the relics of stone, metal, and clay found in connection with them. The interest of such an exemplification of the primeval state of

c

our northern home, we can readily picture ; and to produce such a monument, fairly adjusted and apportioned, is a work such as a body like the
Spalding Club is well calculated to accomplish, and it is worthy of an
effort to achieve.   To prevent its too exclusively absorbing the funds of
the Club, I should think there would be little difficulty in organising an
adequate auxiliary fund, to be subscribed to by volunteers, of whom I
would gladly be one.   I do hope you will think of this as favourably as
I do, and keep the matter in view."

He adds—

" I am just correcting the last sheets of my Theban book.   What re-
ception the volume may meet with I can hardly guess ; but at any rate I
have not spared labour upon it.   To find that it should meet with some
degree of success would naturally, of course, be pleasant, after first toiling
to gather the materials for it in Egypt, and then grinding them into shape
with an amount of labour which it is perhaps as well the result should
not show.   In Edinburgh I hope it will find some readers, who may
already have been interested in the relics in the Museum, which part of
it describes."

This volume, on which Mr Rhind expended so much thought and
labour, was soon afterwards published with the title, " Thebes, its
Tombs and their Tenants Ancient and Present, including a Record of
Excavations in the Necropolis."   It contains eleven chapters, the first
of which is devoted to the general history of Thebes ; the second describes the Necropolis as one of the most remarkable in the world;
the third gives the result of former sepulchral researches ; the fourth
describes the unrifled tomb of a Theban dignitary and its contents,
portions of which were of an unusual character, and others unique ;
the fifth gives an account of a burial-place of the poor ; the sixth
records excavations among tombs of the kings, and of various grades ;
the seventh is devoted to the theories explanatory of Egyptian sepul-
ture ; the eighth to the sepulchral evidence of early metallurgic
practice ; the ninth points out how the demand for Egyptian relics
has been supplied, and its influence on the condition of the monu-

ments; the tenth furnishes an account of the present tenants of the tombs; and the eleventh continues the account of these tenants and of their rulers. The volume is illustrated by plates of the more remarkable objects.

In the preface Mr Rhind explains the delay which had occurred in the appearance of the volume; one reason for which was, his hope of being able to collect a farther series of sepulchral details in other parts of the country.

" But the chief cause of the delay has been that, believing any work intended for publication to be entitled to at least such advantages as time and care may give, the demand for both in this case has been increased by the breaches in continuous progress involved in the circumstances of a lengthened annual absence abroad. Even now I have had to correct the proofs of two-thirds of these sheets about fifteen hundred miles from England."

Mr Rhind is here silent on the subject of interruptions arising from serious illnesses, which at times reduced him to an extreme state of weakness, and permanently disabled him from anything beyond a restricted amount of daily exertion.

On the 5th May Mr Rhind wrote to me from Gibraltar—

" I spent rather more than three weeks in various parts of the island of Teneriffe, but chiefly in the beautiful valley of Orotava, to which Humboldt gave the palm for beauty, even in comparison with all the scenery of the Cordilleras, which he had traversed. I much enjoyed my sojourn there, and in Teneriffe generally. The weather was magnificent, and the climate generally seems to promise so well for a winter, that I am at present minded to return there next year. The facilities of communication with Europe form one considerable inducement, there being six or seven steamers every month. The drawback is the very indifferent accommodation. Another motive to go back is, to investigate a little more fully the relics of the Guanches, the ancient population which the Spaniards found in possession, at the conquest, 400 years ago. Their condition offers some interesting analogies with that of the primeval races of

Europe, &c. ; and what I have already been able to learn on the subject, makes me desirous to have some opportunity of knowing more.   To leave Teneriffe, I took advantage of a mercantile steamer that was to make a long detour, which promised some novelty.   We touched first at another of the Canaries, La Palma, and then at another, Lanzarote—the first mountainous and of considerable beauty ; the last also mountainous, but arid from want of water.   Our next point was Mogador, on the coast of Morocco, where we lay two days.   This town has all the curious oriental characteristics ; but being comparatively new, and having been built as a commercial depôt, it wants much of the picturesqueness of the ancient Muslim cities.   From Mogador we coasted northwards, looking in at three other Barbary towns—Mazagan, Darel Baëes, and Tangier—and arriving here on Friday night, after a pleasant voyage of nine days.   In four and twenty hours I hope to be again under way, as my object is to reach Seville on the 8th, and to stay there until the end of the month. About the beginning of the second week in June, I hope to be at home."

Among Mr Rhind's papers I found a very careful account of Teneriffe, with minute details of its products and resources.   It is a mere fragment, however, and does not touch on the antiquities of the island, his observations on these being probably reserved till after the second visit which he projected.

Mr Rhind resumed his residence at Down House, where he spent the summer of 1862.   In the autumn he was again prostrated by an attack of illness, of which he wrote to me from Clifton on the 20th September.   He had arranged to part with his lease of Down House at this time, with the intention of selecting for next season a more sheltered residence in the same neighbourhood.   In the letter just referred to he writes—

" I have decided to turn my face to Egypt again for the coming winter. I sail for Malta from Southampton on the 4th of next month.   Early in November I hope to be once more on the Nile.   In spring, according to my present plans, I make for Corfu ; and, if strength permits, I intend to get about among the Greek islands for six or eight weeks, with an eye to early vestiges."

Before he left England, Mr Rhind executed a codicil to his settlement, by which he transferred from the University of Edinburgh to the Society of Antiquaries of Scotland his endowment of a Professorship of Archæology. His reasons are fully stated in that document, which is printed in the Appendix to this Memoir.

Mr Rhind reached Egypt in safety, and speedily began a series of systematic observations on the Nile and its deposits. His purpose is thus expressed in a paper found among his notes, which may have been intended as a preface to the volume, which he meant to prepare under the title of " The Nile Valley in Relation to Chronology."

"This work will, with other materials, contain the result of observations made during a voyage devoted to tracing the operations of the Nile for 1000 miles of its course from the second Cataract to the sea. Among the facts embodied are the depth of water ; rate of current ; amount of sediment ; constituents of alluvium and of sand ; these, and other conditions being classified with reference to the respective points in the river's course. Side by side with such data, showing the Nile's mode of action, will be given the various evidences according to their locality of what it has accomplished. Among such evidences are measurements indicating the position of the ancient monuments in relation to the river and the alluvium, and traces of fluviatile action on or near the mountains of the valley. It will be shown from terrace marks in the hills, and the presence of alluvial deposits and river shells at levels high above the present water range, that in its earlier career the Nile was a destructive stream, wearing out its bed where its subsequent work has been to build it up.

" In reviewing the changes which have occurred during the historical period, it will be shown with reference to Lower Nubia and Upper Egypt, that the facts require a different explanation from either of the two most current hypotheses, viz. :—the assumed scooping out of the bed of the river between Semneh and Assouan, or the bursting of a barrier at the rocks of Silsilis. As to Lower Egypt, including the Delta, the subject of the rate of alluvial deposit will be investigated and the value examined of the proofs it may afford as to the antiquity of man's presence."

The following letter to Mr Earle, written from La Majolica, on the Lake of Como, on the 8th of June 1863, is valuable, from its preserving a detailed account of Mr Rhind's proceedings during the previous winter :—

" I do not doubt that, from some of my Clifton friends, you will have long ago learned that there has been only too good reason why I have not replied to your letter, which came to me in Egypt just at the very time of my overthrow. I longed to write to you, but I was unwilling to use another's hand, and I feel that you will forgive me for delaying until I could myself, as it were, speak to you face to face, if it be but a word or two.

" I spent the winter on the Nile pleasantly, and as to health improvingly. But I could not resist getting involved in interesting work, which I could not always keep within proper bounds. The main part of my time was given to investigating the operations of the river and the growth of the alluvium, with reference to the monuments. I began and carried out the work systematically for 1000 miles of the river's course, and had brought my notes and collections into such form, that I had communicated with the Longmans to announce a volume on ' The Nile Valley in relation to Chronology.' When I reached Cairo, I fear I was more diligent mentally and bodily than a due calculation of contingencies warranted ; and one or two detrimental causes having fallen upon me untowardly together, I was prostrated by a sharp attack of hæmorrhage from the lung. I had a weary confinement at Cairo—another at Alexandria. I have been reduced and enfeebled miserably. But yet the necessities of escaping from the heat of the south obliged me to start first for Corfu, which did not at all suit me, and then to journey on until I could halt at this beautiful lake. A week's quiet here has done me some good ; but my exhausted condition of frame, I cannot but see, leaves it doubtful whether the turn of the balance shall be upwards or down. Guided as it will be by the same hand, it will be for me to accept trustfully whatever result the Father bestows.

" In a few days more I hope to make a start to cross the Alps, probably by the Splügen, and to journey, if I am able, to England by slow stages, arriving about the end of the month.

" By the way, I had another piece of work in the winter, which, if it please God that we meet, I should like to have your help with, as it is in your special line of country. I made a vocabulary, and endeavoured to disentangle the grammar of two Nubian dialects, which till now have wanted such exposition. In process of the work I came upon several, and even important facts.

" But, alas! who shall say whether these, and the results of my Nile labours, shall not now return again to chaos. At present I cannot even think consecutively of, much less work at either."

A letter to me from the same place, written on the 5th June, gives much the same account of himself as that just quoted, but with rather less detail. One passage in it may be quoted, to show how warmly he clung to the recollection of old friends.

" In turning over the stranger's book, I saw that Innes spent some time in this house last summer. It reminds me to beg you to remember me to him, and to Robertson. My Cain's doom, I fear, is nearly fatal to my retaining a place in the recollection of friends."

He adds—

" I had not closed this an hour, when a messenger from Como brought me a packet of letters, including yours of the 1st. I feel much your kind remembrance and sympathy. I have not said much about myself in this letter; but you will infer that my condition hangs, as it were, in a balance, and the turn may be to either side. It is for me to bow to the will of the Father, whether His hand shall lead into the sunshine, or into the valley of the shadow."

Mr Rhind's friends could not but be alarmed at such accounts of his health, but he had so often been raised up from a state of great prostration in previous times that hope was not extinguished.

The next accounts, however, brought the intelligence that the end had come, and that the feeble flicker of life had now been extinguished. It was an end serene and beautiful,—in complete unison with the life which preceded it. He literally " fell asleep." The circumstances are detailed in the following letter from Mr Rhind's servant, James Fisher, written to Mr Earle, from Zurich on the 3d of July :—

" You will, I know, be very sorry to hear that poor Mr Rhind is no more; he died sleeping during the night. Yesterday he took a drive, but the heat was so great that he suffered much from it, and complained of being very tired and fatigued when we got back ; and so he determined to go early to bed, and, as he had had a very bad night the previous one, he thought he should be able to sleep better, feeling so tired. At half-past ten I found he was sleeping comfortably. I had to give him some milk, if he awoke during the night, but, as he did not move, I still considered him to be sleeping. I looked at him several times this morning without going near him, thinking I would not wake him ; but at last I stepped quietly up to the bedside, and, to my great horror, found he had ceased to breathe. He must have died without the least struggle—he had not moved his head from the pillow.

" I believe he has written to you since he was first attacked with hæmoptysis at Cairo on the 30th of March. Since then he has never got much stronger ; and although from a three weeks' stay on the Lake of Como he got a very little better, he got worse again by the four days' journey from there to here."

Mr Rhind's body was brought from Zurich, and interred in the family burying-ground in the parish churchyard of Wick, on the 13th of July.

Shortly before the execution of his settlements, in January 1861, Mr Rhind left a letter to his executors, dated 30th November 1860, in which he gave instructions for the completion of his work on the Tombs at Thebes, in the event of his own death before he should have been able to bring it out. He also directed them, in that event, to provide funds for the completion of a volume, containing Fac-similes of two remarkable Bilingual Papyri found by him at Thebes, then in progress, under the charge of Dr Birch, keeper of Oriental Antiquities in the British Museum. This volume was all but finished at the time of his death, and has since been issued with the following title, " Fac-similes of Two Papyri found in a Tomb at

Thebes, with a Translation by Samuel Birch, LL.D., &c.; and an Account of their Discovery, by A. Henry Rhind, Esq., F.S.A., &c. Lond. 1863."

The notes of Mr Rhind's observations and soundings of the Nile, during the early part of 1863, were found among his papers after his death ; but it did not appear that he had completed any part of the volume, of which these were to form the groundwork. While, therefore, these notes could not be printed as a whole, I have thought it right to give in the Appendix extracts containing his observations on the deposits and current of the Nile at Thebes and Memphis, not merely as presenting a remarkable picture of his energetic character and active mind, but as evidences of that *thoroughness* and patience in the pursuit of truth which characterised all his labours, and which now animated him to encounter this long-sustained inquiry at a time of great bodily weakness.

One passage in his observations at Memphis appears very remarkable, not only as a token of his continued appreciation of the value of excavations on historical sites, but also as a testimony to the extent of still unexplored ground in Egypt.

" Deep excavations at Memphis might therefore be very important, as well in a historical as a physical point of view. But, in truth, throughout all Egypt it may be said, that all that has as yet been done in the way of excavation is little more than mere scratching, and the vastness of the mine makes us wonder whether it will ever be thoroughly explored."

It will have been seen that *thoroughness* was the predominating feature of his character, and that it entered into all his pursuits. The study of antiquities with Mr Rhind was a very different thing from the mere gratification of a taste ; whether in the Valley of the Nile, or among the moors of his native Caithness, his search was always for authentic facts and objects, which he reckoned of value

only in their relation to the history of man's progress ; and while
he had every facility and temptation to form a private Museum for
himself, he, from the first, subordinated all his inquiries to public
ends, and placed every object which he could discover or acquire
in a public collection, where classification and accessibility might
render them of real and permanent value. Ever since Mr Rhind
became a Member of the Society of Antiquaries of Scotland, he has
devoted his energies and resources to further its objects and secure
its permanency. There has been no important step in its progress
during the last ten years, in which I cannot trace his influence more
or less directly. He was often prostrated by attacks of severe
illness, but the earliest of his returning powers were devoted to the
furtherance of some work in which the progress of Archæology and
the position of the Society were involved ; and while Mr Rhind
contributed much to its prosperity in his lifetime, the well-considered
bequests with which he has enriched it, show the hearty regard for
its welfare which he maintained to the last. From these it will be
seen, that he has left to the Society his valuable library, which,
after the elimination (suggested by himself,) of a class of works of
a miscellaneous character, not bearing on the objects of the Society,
will still amount to above 1600 volumes, some of them of great rarity
and value. He has left to it a sum of L.400, " to be expended on
practical archæological excavations in the north-eastern portion of
Scotland, where the remains are mostly unknown to the general
student, are often in good preservation, and, from ethnographical
reasons, are likely to afford important information." He gives to
the Society the copywright of his work, " Thebes, its Tombs and
their Tenants," and after providing for the foundation and endowment of an institution at Wick for the industrial training of young
women from certain parishes in the county of Caithness; the foundation of two Scholarships in the University of Edinburgh, and many

other bequests of a private character, he has left the residue of his estate of Sibster for the endowment of a Professor or Lecturer on Archæology in connection with this Society, and has committed its management to the Council, with many practical directions and suggestions, which show how well the subject had been previously considered by him. The last bequest may ultimately yield a sum of about L.7000, but is not available during the lifetime of Mr Bremner, to whom the liferent right of Sibster is left.

It has been a great solace to me to gather up these memorials of our departed friend; but I would not have felt it right to intrude them at such length on the Society if it had not given me the opportunity of preserving many of Mr Rhind's observations and opinions on archæological points, which are of a more general and enduring interest than the mere utterances of private friendship. From the feelings which have been expressed to me, I believe that the members would have felt regret if some such record of the life of one, who has proved so great a benefactor to the Society, had not been preserved, and I cannot doubt, that those who succeed us will be glad to know something of one whose benefactions will bear fruit so long as the Society lasts.

In looking back to the short and bright career of Mr Rhind, it is instructive to observe how much earnest and laborious work he was able to achieve. At the time of his death he had not attained his thirtieth year, and during the portion of his life in which he carried on his historical pursuits, his health was at all times precarious, and often prostrated by severe attacks of illness. Instead, however, of resigning himself to the solaces often necessary, and always captivating to invalids, but which tend rather to enervate than to brace to any great exertion, Mr Rhind pursued his studies with an equable and unbroken ardour—resuming the thread where it had been broken by an attack of illness, and gathering from every country, whither the varying necessities of health carried him, fresh materials for observation and study.

Wherever he went Mr Rhind acquired new friends. To all, his sweetness and unselfishness, his warm and sympathetic nature, could not but be attractive, while to those who could appreciate them, the treasures of his active and-well stored mind formed an additional tie and charm.

A remarkable feature of Mr Rhind's character was his unvarying cheerfulness. He had many alarming illnesses, but he never fretted or became impatient, although for the time he had to abandon some engrossing pursuit. He carried on his labours under a constant sense of his precarious tenure of life, but was never disheartened by it—eager and hopeful while engaged in his favourite pursuits, but implicitly trustful and resigned when warned that he must abandon them. To his unruffled calmness in every contingency we doubtless owe the prolongation of his days, and the many works crowded into a little space, for he seemed to realize the poet's words.

> Not enjoyment and not sorrow
> Is our destined end or way,
> But to act, that each to-morrow
> Find us further than to-day.

While, therefore, we cannot but mourn the early removal of such a friend and associate as Mr Rhind, we mingle with our sorrow admiration of his noble and unselfish character, and cherish as a precious bequest the example of his bright and earnest career.

JOHN STUART.

APPENDIX.

THE NILE VALLEY IN RELATION TO CHRONOLOGY.

THE following extracts from Mr Rhind's MSS., contain his observations and soundings on the Nile at Thebes and Memphis :—

"THEBES, 5th *February* (1863.)—The soundings to-day across the river, abreast of the temple of Luxor *E.* 19. 19. 24. 27. 27. 22. 20. 16. 10. 10. 8. *W.* Here comes an island and another channel which contains water to middle of January.

"The extreme height of the alluvium, or indeed mound above water to-day at the Quay, at south-west corner of temple of Luxor, 20 feet. The pavement of the temple 2·6 below this; therefore 17·6 above water.

"Examined the Shekh (11th February) whose duty it is to note the rise of the river. The appointment, like most others, has been hereditary, and has been long in his family. He himself a man apparently 63 or 65. In the Quay beneath the temple of Luxor, there is a projecting stone, which, in measuring the height of the waters, is reckoned as being 16 drah; that is, theoretically, 16 drah above the lowest Nile, and from all memory has been so held.[1] From this point, therefore, the Shekh begins

---

[1] It would seem, however, that there must be some inaccuracy in this, for, as the facts on the opposite page show, the stone counted 17 drah was 10 feet from the surface of the water, and 17 drah is as nearly as may be 32. Now the deepest soundings on the 5th in the channel, being 27 feet, the 10 feet up to the 17 drah point being added, gives 37. So that if the Shekh's measure starts from low Nile,

to count, and each tier of stone in the quay thereafter is counted as a drah, to which the breadth nearly approximates, namely, about $22\frac{1}{2}$ inches.[1] Two tiers of stones, above that counted 16 drah, only now remain, some of the upper ones (two or three) having within a few years been removed; on measuring from that counted 17 drah to the surface of the water to-day, I found it 10 feet above. According to the Shekh, the Nile rose this (*i.e.* 1862) year $20\frac{3}{4}$[2] drah. This, calculated from the above data, would make it to have been within 1 foot 4 inches of the level of the pavement of the temple. The very high Nile of 1861 was accounted $22\frac{3}{4}$ drah, or about 3·9 higher, which would and did flood the temple by more than 2 feet. On making an excavation at this corner of the temple, I found that the foundation being upon hard impacted alluvium, went down about 8 feet 3 below the level of the pavement. This excavation showed large stones laid regularly at right angles to the wall, and stretching out about 8 feet. At the end of them were some broken fragments of sculptured blocks and others, so that this had probably been part of a building, like a stairs or communication made when the quay was constructed, which is not more than about 50 feet from the temple.

" Shekh Yusuf (he of the water) stated further, that such a Nile as this year is considered fair. But 21 drah is necessary to be a good Nile. Neither of these figures, however, cover all the cultivable land, and about 22 or more is necessary for that. In 1861 the whole was inundated, but he had only four times in his life seen this; in the year (of the
Hegira) 1233—1245—1256—1278. He has known Niles of 18 and
     (1818)   (1830)   (1840)   (1862 ? 1)
19 drah, and has seen ten or twelve years or more at different times, when none, or almost none, of the land was covered. In fact the inundations which naturally command all the alluvium, are here rare. These remarks, derived from Shekh Yusuf's information, it will be observed, relate to the Luxor side.

" The set of the current is on and towards the Luxor side. Its rate, about 80 yards from the bank, was (on 16th February) 100 feet in 22″,

it gives only 5 feet as the then depth, and there would therefore be water in only a very narrow channel.

[1] Some of the lower ones, however, I find to be 20 and 21 inches.

[2] It is worth noting, that at merely special points, the rise of the inundation would vary within periods, according to the changes made in the canals. For example, the cutting of some large ones, a carrying off the water which was formerly to the river's channel. would influence the rise within a given distance below.

being the mean of two trials respectively 20″ and 24″. In the middle of the river, 300 yards further out, the rate was 100 feet in 38″.

"*N.B.*—The rate at which the inundation rises and falls would be an interesting point. It certainly must be in very different ratios at different periods. On the 4th of February I had a mark made at level of water on a stone in the quay at Luxor, and on the 16th I found that the water had only fallen 4 inches and a fraction (say $4\frac{1}{2}$), which would give only at the rate of less than a foot a month. If this were a constant ratio, it would only give a fall of 8 feet during the period of the subsidence of the river, whereas more than 30 feet (?) have to be accounted for, that being the annual rise here. I think there is reason to believe that the rise at Thebes, instead of 36, as stated by Wilkinson, cannot be more than 25 or 26. See on.

" I noted a fact which confirms the Shekh's statement as to the relations of the inundations to the land; opposite Karnak, on that side, the bank is cut by the river into a steep face. The land here between the temple and the river all stands on the level represented by this bank. I found it on the 14th February to be 21 feet 2 inches above the water. Now, calculating from the former data as to the quay, and allowing a difference of 3 inches (according to note above) for the fall in the river as between the dates of the observation here and at the quay, it will be seen that the Nile of 1862 would not have been within 3 feet 5 inches of the top of the bank, while that of 1861 would just have covered it by 7 or 8 inches. When this was the case here, other parts of the plain which are lower would be covered to the depth of 2 or 3 feet, or more; but I found it impossible to obtain precise information showing how this was. Another analogous fact I found, by measuring the depth from the surface of the ground to the surface of the water, in a pit dug for drawing water by shadoofs, about one-third of the way from Luxor to Karnak, and about half a mile from the river. The surrounding land here stands apparently about the same level as that in front of Karnak, at the river where the bank, as above mentioned, was measured. Here likewise the inundation did not reach last year. Accordingly, on measuring to the surface of the water in the pit, I found that it was nearly 21 feet below the surface of the ground in the morning, before the shadoofs were set to work; and this doubtless represents the level of the Nile, for the water in wells dug in the alluvium stands, when undisturbed, as nearly as may be at the height of the river. In the pit here referred to, which was about 8 feet in diameter, at 20 feet deep, I found that by twelve o'clock, when the shadoofs had been working all the morning, the level of the water was lowered by $4\frac{1}{2}$ feet ; but this, or any further diminution, was soon made good by the ooze, when the drawing by the shadoofs ceased for some hours, and the point already mentioned was reached in the morning ; of course the level varies with the rise and fall of the river.   It would seem, and the point is interesting with regard to ancient towns, that everywhere the Nile oozes through its alluvium to a height very nearly corresponding with its level for the time being.   For example, in the plain behind Karnak, there are several depressions, like small dry lakes, perhaps a fourth of an acre less or more in extent, and 8 or 10 feet below the level of the surrounding ground.   From the Fellaheen, who farmed there, I learnt that these fill up to a certain height by ooze, as the river rises, even when the inundation is not sufficiently high to bring water into them from the surface by the flooding from the canals.

" As to wells or shafts sunk for water in the alluvium near the edge of the desert, the conditions are different.   I examined several so situated on the Goorneh side.   In one pit, near Kass E Reebayk, which was cut down through the 3 or 4 feet of superimposed alluvium, and then through the partially concreted sand and pebbles of the desert, I found the water at mid-day 15 feet below the level of the surrounding ground, and in the morning, before the shadoofs begin to work, it stands 2 feet 6 inches to 3 feet higher.   Here, however, the supply came from the desert, and at or about the point at which the water stands in the morning, that is about 12 feet below the surface of the ground, a little rill pours in from the side of the pit next the desert.   I was told that here, and in others similarly circumstanced, the water, although the supply varies, does not rise and fall in correspondence with the Nile.   I measured two others between this and the Memnonium, which are of small diameter, and of the nature of draw-wells, into which buckets descend, and I found the water to be about 14 feet and $13\frac{1}{2}$ respectively below the surface level. As the covering of alluvium over the desert is not very thick here, the height of the water in those wells will probably depend upon the supply from the desert.   If it were not so, or if other wells existed somewhat further out in the alluvium, in which the water, being ooze from the Nile, would stand approximated at its level, the measurement from the surface of the water in them, to the surface of the ground above, would have been a ready means of showing whether the land here is on the same level, or lower than nearer the river.

The plain of Thebes, in relation to the Nile, may be held to be in most respects a fair representative of the state of the case generally throughout

Upper and Middle Egypt, and the details which it offers are more pointed and indicative from the presence of some of the monuments in very significant positions. In the first place, a glance at the map will readily show the main features. The valley, at the point where it is necessary first to note it with reference to the Theban plain—the valley here, that is, about three miles south of Luxor, is somewhat narrowed, the distance from mountain to mountain being perhaps from six to eight miles. From this breadth, however, it immediately expands as Thebes is approached, and the measurement across, in a line with the ruins of Karnak, would not be much less than twelve miles, of which three-fourths may be allowed for the river, three for the alluvium on the Goorneh side, six for that on the Karnak side, counting both at their broadest, and from two to three for the low slopes of the desert at the foot of the mountains on both sides. The course of the river, in flowing through this part of the valley, is somewhat oblique, which generally characterises its line of progress through the lower country, as it winds from one reach to another. At the southern point, about three miles above Luxor, already specified, its channel nearly approaches the eastern desert, but presently trending towards the opposite side, it sweeps up to the western desert six miles lower down. The plain is thus cut into two unequal portions, of which that upon the Goorneh side is less than half of the other. Besides the main channel, it is necessary, from their influence on the irrigation, also to notice those lateral offshoots from it which, for about six months of the year, form three islands situated respectively above Luxor, opposite Luxor, and in front of Karnak. The former of these, or rather the channel which insulates it, is the most important. Indeed, there is reason to believe, from the direction of the ancient quay at the south-west corner of the temple of Luxor, which now abuts upon this channel, that at one time the main stream may have flowed in very nearly the same line. But supposing that to have been the case, the channel in question, like so many other parts of the river, has been the subject of changes since. In the first place, it must have become a subsidiary branch; and, again, it has cut with a deeper curve northwards, so that its sweep is now behind the line of the quay; and its tendency appears to have been to enlarge its bed. But within the last fifteen or twenty years it is stated by residents to be conveying less water than formerly, some silting up, or change of current, at the point where it branches off from the main stream, directing no doubt more of the water into the latter. Alterations of this kind are almost everywhere, and always going on. This channel, however, is still an important one at high Nile, although nearly dry at the end of February; and from it run the

D

lines of several canals, which, although with one or two exceptions now old and inefficient, help to bring the waters of the inundations over large portions of the plain. A reference to the plan will readily show how the canal system operates to accomplish this. Skirting the edge of the desert may first be observed the line of one large canal, intended to benefit an extensive district. Its mouth, whence it receives its supply as the river rises, is a few miles above the plain of Thebes; and it fringes the culti-vated land as far as Koos, a distance of some twenty miles, whence down-wards other similar works carry on the same purpose. Embanked on the desert side it throws the inundation forward on the plain, and its chan-nel being suitably sluiced towards its lower extremity, the waters may be dammed up, so that even with a moderate Nile the land is flooded. This canal, which irrigates all the back district of the Theban plain, has been cut within the last few years. Till then, that is, referring to modern times, the work was done less efficiently by smaller conduits, of which I have inserted one in the plan, being that which is now mainly operative in irrigating the ground towards the centre of the plain, too far from the large canal to be within its influence. This conduit canal enters from the channel already described. It winds, often with a very serpentine course, to the eastward of Karnak, or in the direction of Medamoot, and, being embanked on both sides, it is made to convey the water through breaches in the dikes over the fields on either hand.

In this way the main area of the plain between Karnak and the desert is, except with a very low Nile, annually irrigated. For the immediate neighbourhood of Karnak, and the tract between it and the river, a cer-tain provision to facilitate the rise of the water has been made by some small canals brought up more or less obliquely from the river; but it is only with what they call a very good Nile that they are of much use. In fact, all the space lying along the margin of the river, from Luxor to Karnak, and the district about and in front of Karnak, have, it may be said, not more than the natural irrigation to depend upon, and are inun-dated only when the Nile itself clears its banks. The rarity with which this effectually occurs may be inferred from the fact already stated, that only four times within the last forty-five years has the whole cultivable land, situated as above described, been covered by the water.

On the Goorneh side the irrigation is now chiefly effected by one large canal, which, entering at Erment, runs on to Gamoola. The portion of the plain between it and the river has principally to depend for its inun-dation upon the rise of the latter, and as a certain breadth of the land here is on a gradual slope to the water, a large part of it is usually covered every year. When, however, this upward slope ends in the level which represents the high ground in the plain, this, just as on the Karnak side, is above the reach of the ordinary overflow, and this year a considerable strip along the dike of the canal was not flooded—that is, the height of the Nile could not reach it.

Between the canal and the desert, however, the land was abundantly overflowed; and it must be a very low Nile indeed with which this could not be accomplished; for on its eastern margin the canal is embanked to a height of from 8 to 10 feet, so as to throw the water forward. In the plain so treated are the Colossi, and the buried substructures of three temples; and on the line where it bounds with the desert stand the great ruins of Medineet Haboo, the Memnonium, and Kasr E Rubayk. Each and all of these are now subjected in different degrees to the inundations. The Colossi are surrounded by it, the substructures of the three temples are covered by it, and a high Nile, such as that of 1861, encroaches upon the others which have been named. In Kasr E Rubayk the water that year stood to a height of about 2 feet.

Not only are these vestiges now subject to the range of the inundation, but, as a natural consequence, the alluvium has encroached upon them in varying degrees, according to their position. The Colossi, which of these monuments stand the most forward in the plain, have at various times (?) been examined with reference to this encroachment; and it has been found that the alluvium now stands 6 feet 10 inches above the pavement of the avenue which passed between them. The highest water-mark upon them was likewise shown to be about 10 inches above the alluvium; and since the cutting of the new canal it is higher still—the water having, with the ordinary Nile of this year, gained fully one foot beyond this point, while in 1861, according to the accounts I received, it was fully 2 feet more, making in all a height of nearly 11 feet above the pavement. Now, in the first place, it may fairly be assumed, that when the temple (whose substructures are now covered by the soil) was built, to which this avenue led, neither it nor the statues which adorned the approach to it were likely to be so placed that the annual inundation would flood them. But, on the other hand, the extent to which this now occurs, and the thickness of the superincumbent alluvium, can give no general criterion as to the results of the river's operation in the interval. For *first*, It will be seen how much the presence of the irrigation, and consequently the growth of alluvium, is under the influence of artificial means. *Second*, It cannot be known whether, by dikes or other contrivances which may have long been in use to protect Thebes as a city before the Colossi were raised, the inundations had been so far kept out that their site may at that time have been under the level that otherwise would have been subject to the natural operations of the river, and that, therefore, when these were allowed play when Thebes decayed, the alluvium soon increased here in a greater than its normal ratio. *Third*, Or conversely, we do not know how far above the normal line of alluvium the level of the pavement may have been at the time of its construction, and therefore we cannot say whether the present alluvium above it represents the whole increase since then or not. *Fourth*, There is no possibility of learning what may have been from time to time, since the fall of Thebes, the varying system of agriculture, and particularly of irrigation here,—whether, at certain periods, there may not have been such canals as that recently made on the one hand, or, on the other, inferior arrangements, which would have made the inundations over this ground, and therefore the deposit, be greater or less at different times, and so frustrate all calculation as to rate of increase.

"MEMPHIS, *March* 8, Bedushayn.—The alluvial valley, from the river to the edge of the desert, may be about 4 miles broad, and the mounds of Memphis, covering a vast space, lie about midway across. The irrigation of the land, which seems very completely effected, is mainly accomplished from the Bahr Yousef, which is dammed up at a bridge, as described in the previous case. Minor channels and dikes are brought into play to spread the waters; and these channels, which often have the character of new depressions, deprive the valley here, as in most cases where it is broad, of a dead-level appearance, and irregularities, with water resting in hollows, frequently present themselves. The irrigation of the back district, being independent of the Nile's local rise, it may be said never fails; but the tract immediately along the bank, perhaps half a mile or more wide, was not overflowed this year. And the bank here, over which the water did not pass, was 17 feet 10 inches above the water to-day. The ground about the mounds of Memphis is certainly not so high, according to what seems to be the principle that the valley towards the desert is lower : and, indeed, there are tracts of the back district here (not however immediately around Memphis) which are not on a higher level than 8 or 10 feet above the surface of water still left in the canals. I measured one well west from Memphis (about a quarter of a mile), in which the water was barely 8 feet below the average surrounding surface. In the mounds of the town, the old brick houses, or substructures of the lower ones, are sometimes seen in strata, as it were, of different heights, showing the growth of one age succeeding another. The only point offering some record of the progress of the alluvium here is beside the prostrate colossal statue of Ramses II. The excavation of the nature of a trench, which had been made to disclose it, had uncovered at its feet the lower portion of a building, being either part of a pedestal on which it may have stood, or of a structure with which it had been connected. This building, so far as it is discernible, consists of two courses of massive stones, the upper being laid a few inches within the perpendicular line of the other, in the manner in which a superstructure above ground is made to rest upon the last course of the foundation. As even now there was water in the trench, I could not have it cleared for an examination still deeper of the fabric. But if we take the date of the prostrate statue to indicate that of the building, and if we assume the top of the lower course to represent the then ground surface, it will be found that the following are the data for the increase of the alluvium. From the top of the course in question, to the level of the irrigation, this year was about 9·8, and the general level of the nearest cultivated flat may be stated at about 2 feet less; so that the actual thickness of alluvium over the old surface line is very nearly 8 feet. Nor can it be supposed that this represents all the increase since the days of Ramses II., for it cannot be imagined, that when the temple was built its pavement was laid on the level of the natural surface, and just clear of the irrigation. On the contrary, its site would be most likely to have some elevation,[1] and whatever we conceive this elevation to have been, we must add its amount to the eight feet to get at the gain of the alluvium within the period in question. But on the other hand, there comes into play the consideration referred to in the case of Thebes, that we do not know whether the site of Memphis, at the period when the building in question was erected, may not have been under the normal local level of the alluvium, artificial arrangements having, perhaps, existed, whereby the inundation for a long course of years had not been allowed to operate. In this case, the accumulation of the alluvium, when the protecting care was withdrawn, would be more than normally rapid. But there is always a comparatively narrow limit to any supposition of the site of the Town being much lower than the influence of the irrigation, for even if the latter were banked out, the nature of the soil is such, that any depression would be rendered for a certain period of the year a swamp by the ooze. From this it may be held to follow, that when a massive building like that to which the portion in question belonged was to be built, at least a firm site would be sought, or artificially made for it ; and it would seem to be conclusive, that its pavement would be so

[1] *Note.*—As to urging excavation *below* ruin of Memphis.

high, that whatever alluvium is now above it must be held as representing a normal growth, at least equal to its own thickness. This reasoning would not apply so well, or at all to the Colossi, as they are founded upon the desert where the filtration would not be operative, as in the case of Memphis, which stood upon the alluvial plain. It is particularly worthy of remark, that the peculiarity of Memphis would make deep excavations on its site exceedingly interesting. For, considering that the lower part of buildings presumed to be of the date of Ramses II. are now buried to the depth of eight feet, and flooded by the inundation; and considering that the same processes were likewise in operation earlier, it might be, looking to the reputation which Memphis always possessed of a vast antiquity, that traces of older structures still lie at lower levels. As the years of the city advanced, that imperceptible surface-growth of *debris* which is generally found to have gone on in ancient towns, would be ever stimulated by the relation of the soil to the inundations, and when older buildings fell into decay, the fate of at least their substructures would be to be covered over by builders of later ages. Deep excavations at Memphis might therefore be very important, as well in an historical as a physical point of view. But in truth, throughout all Egypt, it may be said that all that has as yet been done in the way of excavation, is little more than mere scratching, and the vastness of the mine makes us wonder whether it will ever be thoroughly explored. In the alluvium, westward from Memphis—that is, on the edge of the desert at Sakkara—there are depressions, and particularly one, where the water lodges even at present. The ground is apparently low hereabout. Sir G. Wilkinson's idea is, that the river may anciently have flowed here, and he refers to the statement of Herodotus as to Menes turning the channel at a certain distance above Memphis. But whether any such statement of Herodotus as to a time and personage so obscure is worthy of an attempt at verification, the channel, whether originally natural or artificial, of what is now the Bahr Yousef, no doubt found its way down somewhere near the desert. The present line of the Bahr Yousef is somewhat further out in the plain. But nearer the desert a raised dike which traverses the plain, and is formed from the earth dug out at its feet, is very plentifully strewed with dead shells (*Cyrene consobrina*[1] and others) brought up with the soil. This probably indicates, if not the presence of a considerable water course, a more marshy condition along this tract."

---

[1] As to the relation of the *Cyrene* to the river, note that I have observed great quantities of the shell (*Cyrene*) tolerably fresh, *i.e.*, with colour, in the heap alongside a

II.—MR RHIND'S BEQUESTS TO THE SOCIETY OF ANTIQUARIES OF SCOTLAND.

By his Will Mr Rhind conveyed to Alexander Kincaid Mackenzie, Manager of the Commercial Bank of Scotland, Edinburgh ; David Bremner, of Her Majesty's Customs, Aberdeen ; Alexander Wares, Agent for the Union Bank in Wick ; and John Stuart of the General Register House, Edinburgh, as his trustees and executors, his estate of Sibster, in Caithness, and all his other property.

After many bequests to relations and friends, Mr Rhind leaves a sum of L.5000 for the foundation of two scholarships in the University of Edinburgh, and L.7000 for the establishment at Wick of an Institution for the Industrial Training of Orphan Girls from certain parishes in the county of Caithness.

His bequests to the Society are in the following terms :—

I.—BEQUEST OF £400 FOR EXCAVATIONS.

" And further, I direct my trustees to pay four hundred pounds to the Society of Antiquaries of Scotland, to be expended in practical archæological excavations in the north-eastern portion of Scotland, where the remains are mostly unknown to the general student, are often in good preservation, and from ethnographical reasons are likely to afford important information—and I point more particularly, but not exclusively, to the upland districts of the counties of Caithness, Sutherland, and Ross ; and the said Society shall be at liberty to delay the expenditure of the said bequest for ten years after they receive it, allowing it or any portion of it to accumulate, so as to wait for an opportunity for making a grant or grants to a competent person or persons who would be willing to lay out the whole of such grants for actual excavation, so that none, if possible, would be diverted for personal expenses : declaring that it is also a condition that the said Society shall publish the results of such excavations, duly illustrated, in their Transactions, or in any way they may determine ;

small branch canal near the Abbassëah (Cairo), just at the boundary of the cultivated land and the desert. This heap constituted either what had been in the trench originally, if it were a new one, or the scourings, if old. The distance to the Nile from the spot is rather more than four miles, but there is a large canal within a quarter of a mile.

but I recommend a substantive volume to be published under their auspices and issued by subscription or otherwise, for with this in view, the excavations would be more systematically undertaken, and the archæological data from a given district would be rendered more available by being brought together in one focus."

II.—BEQUEST OF LIBRARY.

" I give and bequeath to the Society of Antiquaries of Scotland, my library—that is to say, all the books that I may die possessed of; but as the condition hereby attached to this bequest is, that my library, from containing mostly works of a cognate character, shall be added to and preserved with the library of the said Society, but not kept apart or in any way distinguished except by the insertion of a book-plate shewing them to have been a bequest, I point out, and trust to the discretion of their Council that they will separate these books of mine which are of a miscellaneous or otherwise unsuitable character for the library of the said Society, and the books so separated I hereby bequeath to the said David Bremner."

III.—BEQUEST FOR FOUNDING A PROFESSORSHIP OF ARCHÆOLOGY.

" Whereas, In my said will and explanatory document relative thereto, I bequeathed to the Senatus or other competent governing body of the University of Edinburgh, a sum from the reversion of the estate of Sibster for the endowment of a Chair of Archæology and History in the said University, and as I have since become aware of the alterations in that University in operation or proposed under the recent Act, involving the endowment of the existing Chair of History and other changes, I conceive that my object will be better fulfilled by bequeathing the said reversionary sum, which I hereby bequeath accordingly in trust to the Council of the Society of Antiquaries of Scotland for a similar, to wit, the following purpose :—The said reversionary sum shall be securely invested for all time coming, and the annual interest accruing thereupon shall be paid to a lecturer, reader, or professor of archæology (according to whichever title may be selected by the said Council), the election of which lecturer shall be vested in and be made by the said Council, as the objects I have in view are two,— *First*, To assist in the general advancement of knowledge ; and *Second*, To aid in furnishing some suitable positions of moderate emolument for students, which positions are now so greatly wanting in Scotland. I believe the latter of these objects will be equally well accomplished by the establishment of a lectureship as above, in connexion with the Society of Antiquaries of Scotland, while the former object will, upon the whole, be more appropriately carried out, as the scope of a lectureship in archæology and allied subjects might be more discursive than might seem altogether to accord with systematic University teaching. I hereby therefore revoke the bequest of the said reversionary sum to the said University, and bequeath the said sum for the said purpose in trust to the Council for the time being of the said Society of Antiquaries of Scotland, declaring that it shall be a condition in their appointment of the said lecturer or professor that he shall be bound to deliver annually a course of not less than six lectures on some branch of archæology, ethnology, ethnography, or allied topic, in some suitable place; but declaring also that the said Council shall determine whether entry to the said lectures shall be gratuitous to the public or by some moderate payment, the proceeds of which shall be delivered to the said Society of Antiquaries, or added to the said lecturer's emolument; and declaring further, that the said Council shall have power to decide all other details, and to decide whether the appointment to the said lectureship shall be for life or for a term of years : And if at any time it shall appear to the said Council that the said lectureship should have a larger endowment than the sum herein bequeathed may provide, the said Council shall be at liberty to request and accept donations or bequests to a fund for that purpose; and I hereby declare, to guard against error, that the sum from the proceeds of the estate of Sibster bequeathed by me in my foresaid will and relative document to the Senatus or other competent body of the said University of Edinburgh for the establishment of scholarships, is not affected by these presents.

IV.—By a letter of instructions to his trustees as to papers and other literary matters, he directs them to provide funds for the completion of his book entitled "Thebes : its Tombs and its Tenants." The letter contains the following passage :—"I hereby declare that any profits [from the sale of the volume] shall belong to the Society of Antiquaries of Scotland, and that the copyright of the volume shall be their property."

www.ingramcontent.com/pod-product-compliance
Lightning Source LLC
Chambersburg PA
CBHW030853260626
47169CB00008B/2519